HEADQUARTERS ABERDEENSHIRE
LIBRARIES

2 5 NOV 2011

0 8 DEC 2012 WITHDRAWN
FROM LIBRARY

- 1 JUL 2013

HEADQUARTERS

D1345538

19 MAR 2014 ABERDEENSHIRE
LIBRARIES
HEADQUARTERS

3 1 JUL 2014 WITHDRAWN
FROM LIBRARY

18 AUG 2015

HEADQUARTERS

- 3 APR 2017 ABERDEENSHIRE
LIBRARIES

**ABERDEENSHIRE LIBRARY
AND INFORMATION SERVICE
MELDRUM MEG WAY, OLDMELDRUM**

Paine, Lauran, 1916-

The outcast / Lauran
Paine

WES

1131063

A L I S

1131063

THE OUTCAST

He saw it as he came out of the arroyo—a sickening redness of the lowering sky. There was a running sore of flame and wreckage against the deep-brooding night. The cabin and barn were blazing!

He saw it with a stunned horror that was almost suffocating. He ran and ran.

His father was outside, face down, sprawled and shot dead. Shot three times.

His never saw his mother, for she was in the log house. But he knew what had happened to her.

THE OUTCAST

Lauran Paine

This hardback edition 1999
by Chivers Press
by arrangement with
Golden West Literary Agency

Copyright © 1950 by Lauran Paine in the
British Commonwealth
Copyright © 1999 by Lauran Paine

All rights reserved

ISBN 0 7540 8064 1

British Library Cataloguing in Publication Data available

WES
113063

Printed and bound in Great Britain by
Redwood Books, Trowbridge, Wiltshire

Chapter One

He stood there in the hot black earth looking out at the dark sweep of land that had on it a twilight depth of softness. A man in an old grey shirt with faded pants, with one gun around his middle and the carbine standing beside him under his careless hand—watching the sun as it went lower over the distances with a great, spreading flame both blood and gold.

To the north were blue shadows falling over the burnt-dry hills. Westward was the tang of an ancient dagger that was sputtering sunlight made savage and vicious before its dogged retreat into the belly of the Universe.

South were the rain forests, and behind him too, so that purple was the clothing colour of the uplands. He had strode out of them to stand up there, transfixed; watching the land he had been foaled in. A vast unfurling of raw distances below, ahead and northward from him. Behind him in the rain forests was security for the hunted.

He was the hunted.

He had no thought for the tiredness weighing heavily on his twenty year old frame nor for the hollow gut of him that trembled for food. He had no glance for the maize-yellow of the sunsplashes, either. Nor for the saffron hills quick-turning and seeming to writhe in the failing light. He saw it all and yet, in a way, he saw none of it. The beauty was a stirring thing; a living symbol of this lost land beyond the law of men and nations and cleaving unto its own with a bitter pride and a quick fierceness.

Below, where the last of the mountainous out-fall levelled off, was a heavy house, low and ugly. A thing of this land where strength counted and life was vivid. Where hardship was commonplace and laughter was a thing to be hoarded.

He stood like a sentinel waiting for the last of the light to die. He let his slow glance caress the nearness of that squat log house.

There was the barn with its proud height and silent strength. It had shielded and fed and—yes—even hidden, animals and men. There was the out-house, a square building of tight dimensions and ugly utility. Inside were the leaching vats where he had helped make soap out of the winter's store of food-fats. He had early developed the knack of breathing through his mouth when he took fat to the vats, for the stench was a rancid, nauseating thing, thick and cloying. Then, when the moon was in the right quarter, the boiling and the stirring in of wood ashes; the shaping and handling of the new bars.

And the house. There would be a fire on the great stone hearth. He remembered that best. The fire and the way it made the laboriously honed inner wall of logs and punched-in mud and moss a roseate, soft red warmth of dullness.

The fire, and his uncle reading the Book to his brood with the walls red-dull and drowsy. Thick; mightly protecting the people of that family.

His uncle with the thick, fiery beard and the square hewn face with its might and its bluntness. His aunt with her expression of deep stillness. Her way of watching, of looking at a person as though she saw clean through them. And her large, long hands with the veins showing through blue and corded. Hands with a power of tenderness in them; a way of slight-deftness that soothed and salved and saved.

6

And there was Caleb—Cal—and Jason, called Jay. His own cousins but not his equal in quickness. Only in their broad, squat bulk and their stamina; in the strength of their shoulders and the hawk-like soundness of their eyes, could they equal him. Sound, hard boys, thoughtful and with a need for release within them.

He thought of all the people and of all the other times when he had hayed with them and branded and whooped and thundered after their cattle with them—and he waited, for the sun was yet high.

Waited—he had a knack of that. It had come hard, for he wasn't a patient man, but he had learned patience well. So he stood up there seeing everything and nothing, for the land was drowsy and summer-burnt with a crispness of fall in the air after sundown—and he waited.

There wasn't a lift of dust anywhere. No riders, nothing. It was safe to go down. The rumbling behind his shell-belt became more insistent. It sent up an acidity into his throat that was bitter and unpleasant. He spat—and waited. Then the last rays died and the hush part of the twilight was on the land.

He started back into the trees to his horse. The animal was travel-stained and gaunted-up, but he was shiny with health and alert of eye and ear. He was a good horse for a hunted man to ride.

He swung up and slid the carbine into the boot under his leg. The way was smooth with pine needles to the edge of the trees, then downward swiftly over the cured grass, downward to the creek behind the ugly log house where the katydids made their croaking sounds and the trees were stalwart among the willows. There he tied up and left the horse.

Instinct made him wince from the open places. His route to the rear door was a series of angling digressions, with cover ahead and retreat behind. Then, under the pole overhang, he smelt the richness of life-giving food coming out through the cracks. It made the saliva run fast. He balled up a fist and struck the door.

It was a muted sound, deep and resonant. From within came an abrupt stillness, then he heard his uncle say: "Shroud the lamp, Jem." He waited with a depth of uncertainty in him, then the door was opening. He saw the squat, powerful build of his kinsman.

"Uncle Zack. It's Lew."

There was a second's silence, then a ragged outletting of a long breath. "Lew. You can't stay here, boy."

It was like cold water over a hot body. A kick in the stomach from a gentle horse. "I'm hungry, Uncle Zack."

"Food," his uncle turned his head a little so that the firelight from the hearth shone coppery on his fierce beard. "Jem, wrap up some meat in a cloth. It's Lew." Then the square hewn head turned and the eyes, with their cloudy look, gazed fully into his face. "They've been here, Lew, lookin' for you. Boy—I hate doing this like I hate anything I've ever done. There's your Aunt Jem and my boys, Lew. I dassn't give you aid or they'll be down on us, too."

"I'll ride," Lew said softly. "I was hungry is all." And he was; the hunger as much of the heart as of the stomach.

"Come inside, Lew; out of the light."

He did, and Zack closed the door with a hand that was white-knuckled on the draw-bar. He saw Jay first, standing like a statue, looking at him. And Cal over by his mother—he was very much like her in most ways—and Jemima Bullard, called Aunt Jem. She worked swiftly with the least of motions so that every motion counted. Cold beef and half a lean roast of deer meat, four sweeps and a knot on top and it was done.

She walked over to him looking directly into his face with the deep, penetrating way she had of looking at people —then she smiled at him.

"It's been a long time, Lew."

"Fifteen months," he said swiftly.

She held his glance in her own and said no more. Zachary Bullard was still holding the draw-bar of the door. His eyes were full of pain and uneasiness—things that make for rebellion.

Lew smiled down into her face and thanked her. There was still a little time left. He knew, if his uncle did not, that there was no one abroad. He knew it from the long vigil up on the high slope.

"Cal, you're lookin' good."

Cal looked flushed and uncomfortable. He made a quick smile and moved his hands futilely. "About like always, Lew. Miss you around at brandin' time."

He nodded and looked to the doorway where the rich glow of the fire made the walls dull red. "Jay—"

"Lew," Zack said in a troubled way, "have you been over in the valleys?"

"Yes; there and other places, Uncle Zack."

"What did you see?" The blue eyes with their anxiety were fixed on his face.

"They are everywhere," Lew said. "They've killed more people and burned houses. The valley folks are leavin'. They're going to the rendezvous south of St. Joseph in the cane-brakes."

"Going to Zion," Zack said softly.

Lew nodded, watching his uncle's face, seeing the anguish there. "Overland," he said.

"It's a bad time of the year, Lew."

There was no answering that, but there was an oblique irony to offer. He offered it. "Have they a choice? The gentiles are ridin' every night. It's getting worse." He almost said 'your time's coming,' but he didn't. "They're ranging farther and farther out. It's even got so's the gentiles say anyone they got a grudge against is a Mormon."

9

He remembered something he'd heard Elder Mortonson say once : 'The sun is down in this land for us.' He remembered it, but didn't say it.

Cal and Jay were graven images with wet eyes. Aunt Jem never looked away from his lean toughness; from the sunburnt, tawny, half-wild look of him. "Lew," she said quietly, "will they come over here?"

"They've been here looking for me, haven't they? Well, they know we're kin. They may even know you're Mormons."

"Leave off," Zachary said gruffly. "We're out of it, Jem. We're a long way off."

Lew's lower cheeks rippled. He had to fight back the hot words, and the silence grew among them until his uncle broke it again.

"I've never blamed you, Lew, although it wasn't the Lord's way. A man's lot is hard at best. I've never judged you—nor will I." He lifted up his glance to the younger man. "My way may seem wrong to you; someday you'll have a family. Then you'll understand, I reckon." He paused again. "Where will you go now?"

"To St. Joseph, I reckon. To Zion. There's nothing here for me but a gentile hang-rope." Lew regarded his mother's brother with a curious gaze. In his own heart he was at peace—and yet he was a hunted man. Zachary Bullard was a man at peace—and yet his heart was troubled. It was ironic. It should have been the other way around. "Uncle Zack, what I did a lot of men have done. I know—that doesn't make it right. I would do it again." He held the packet of food the tighter under his arm next to his lean, gaunt ribs. "I hope none of you are ever put to the same test."

Zachary Bullard remained silent with his eyes chest-level and waiting. Lew knew the sign. He straightened up and smiled at Aunt Jem, looked swiftly at Jay and Cal and moved to the door. Zachary held it open for him. A wisp of a chill groped in out of the darkness. They all felt it and smelt the fragrance of the troubled land in it, as well.

"Lew? Go with our blessing, son."

That was Aunt Jem. He nooded at her and went. Uncle Zack closed the powerful door and Lew heard the draw-bar drop into its hanger. It was as though that small sound was cutting him off from the known world of his childhood and early manhood.

He went back to his horse, mounted and rode around the ranchyard and down across the land. Distantly, behind him, he heard an owl hoot twice, after the fashion of owls. There was a quick answer.

He reined up, listening. The last hoot had rung false in his ears. He sat stock-still with a tightness of gnawing fear within him. The Indian signal. Moments dripped by and nothing more came out of the darkness. He let out a long-held breath. The distance might have distorted the sound. Anyway, there was no further noise.

He lifted the reins and went on again, feeling within Aunt Jem's bundle, tearing slabs of meat with his fingers and wolfing them down; restoring his man's-strength.

And riding, his mind went back.

*　　*　　*　　*

His father's corn patch with the dull red sky over it. The lull that always came in the late fall evenings between sundown and night. The lanky boy standing there in ragged homespun. A sweaty kid, smudged and dirty from building little faggot cones for a smudging fire. A waiting kid, sniffing the night air; waiting for the last minute before he lit the faggot piles so's the frost wouldn't kill the corn. Watching the rim of the world just above the treetops.

There was only sky, like blood, up there—then he felt the sharp, fierce sting in the air. Frost was coming to-night. He laughed aloud and the sound had startled him. Until then he hadn't been conscious of the drowning hush over everything. Being a mile and better from the house, there wouldn't be any sound.

He felt like a general who had outwitted a savage, cruel foe. He waited, savouring; then, when the frigid hosts had come a-stealing down out of the trees, he went slowly, insolently, from one faggot pile to another, bent with his triumphant smile, and lighted each one. He could almost see the shock, the consternation and repulse of the hosts of white-death. He laughed again and felt wonderfully proud, too, for this had been his job and his alone, and he had done it well.

His father had been away for two days helping some neighbours who were moving on west, and when he had come home, his grey eyes had been moist and red looking. There had been an inwardness to the vacant glance.

"Lew son; go make smudges and fire 'em. There's a feel of frost in the air."

He'd watched his father go into the log house. He'd seen the strange, long, mute look his parents had exchanged in the kitchen, then his father had dropped like a stone on the old bed, exhausted, worn and used-up looking.

He'd done it. He'd proven himself in that cornfield. He watched his "skunks" burn and reluctantly he turned to walk back through the rain forest. He had gone out a boy and was returning a man.

The gloomy, brooding forest plucked at him with its sad loneliness. He thought of the Indians who had lived there, but it frightened him thinking like that, so he thought of his mother. That was different, for she was comfort and solace to him. He wondered if she'd let him go over to Uncle Zack's again the coming spring. He'd ask her. He'd do it that very night.

Thinking of his mother made him abruptly uneasy, for he'd seen her cry lately. And twice he'd come upon her when she looked hurt in the eyes. Embarrassment at such a frightening show of womanly weakness had made him tongue-tied about it. But he'd ask her about that, too. They were close. All three of them were close, but Lew and his mother were the closest. He would ask her.

The path out of the trees swung downward into a baffled little arroyo that had turned itself almost inside out trying to become flat-land again. He followed the deer-trails. The smell of smoke was still strong. Casually, he wondered at that. Surely his "skunks" wouldn't smell *this* far off. Oh —but they were strong and well made "skunks." Yet it was strange on so still a night . . .

He saw it when he came out of the funny little arroyo. A sickening redness to the lowering sky. A running-sore of flame and wreckage against the deep-brooding night.

The cabin and log barn in flames!

He saw it with a stunning horror that was almost suffo-cating. He ran, making small sounds he didn't know he made. Ran and ran—and ran.

A lean, lanky man-boy diminutive before the wrath of the fire that writhed and swore and beckoned to him, then forced him back with its awful heat and pummelled him unmercifully, terribly, with its breath.

His father was outside, face down, sprawled and dead. The long rifle with its hickory stock was broken and smashed beside him as though someone had lifted it high and dashed it against the earth. Shot three times and dead.

He never saw his mother, for she was in the log house. But the smell told him, and he dropped down like a stone beside his father and might have been dead but for the faint lifting and falling of his old shirt.

And why? Because they were Mormons! . . . Damned Mormons! . . .

*　　*　　*　　*

The shock lay deep in his remembering blood. The

pain was a depth in his heart; a vacant depth of stillness; a loneliness that was bottomless as he rode away into the rain forests and lived there, a hunted thing who came out but three times.

Each time a gentile had died terribly. Three times the wraith a-horseback had come down into Kelso County and sought out a man. Gerald Knight first, then Herkimer Blount, and lastly, their old neighbour, Foote Garland. A spectre with a blazing gun—-Lewis Moses Landsborough : Mormon !

It had been a simple thing to find out who had done it. All a ragged, sick boy had done was listen, for gentiles bragged of crimes against Saints. But afterward there was hardship, not just for Lew but for everyone. Strife and bloodshed. The hunters and the hunted. Down the years, gathering a momentum of hatred until it became a seething, tortured tide of humanity small and beset, like ants, across the huge bosom of the land. The persecuted and the persecutors. The hunters and the hunted.

He rode away from the Bullard place thinking all the jumbled, terrible things that had followed him across those days and nights. A lean man on a gaunt horse eating chunks of half-cooked meat in the night. In the evening vapours. He smiled a little. Evening vapours. His mother used to say a person should stay well inside after sundown because the evening vapours brought fevers. He couldn't tell her what he'd found out since—that they didn't at all.

There was a pretty little creek nearby. He remembered it well and sought it out. In the summer it was willow-lined and flowery. In the faint moonlight it was silver-white and shone with a strange, sad irridescence.

He stopped and let the horse drink and snuffle, went upstream a little, lay flat and drank, too. Drinking, he thought how it would look when the pre-dawn came. Those vapours as white as watered milk, nearly transparent, scudding low over the prairie. Drifting upwards in the first cold sunlight. Things would stir in the new day; in the sky and on the prairies. In the very waters of this creek. Well, he would be across the flatland into the foothills by then.

He raised himself, feeling full and surfeited and perilously drowsy. He got to his haunches and looked broodingly up at the tattered old tapestry of sky with its moth-holes where light showed through. Mormon Heaven up there. A place for the Saints. A place for weary men and hunted men.

Elder Mortonson had said " . . . yea; the time cometh, that whosoever killeth you will think that he doeth God service." He had said that to Lew.

His face twisted a little on that. The time cometh all right. It was here and now. He started to rise off his haunches with a chip of steely bitterness hurting his soul and his eyes tawny and tired like the eyes of an old wolf. And he heard horsemen coming . . .

A rough hand over the black's nose, poised to clamp down. A man's heart beating like a wild thing enchained and his face a knot of fear and dread and defiance. Riders in the late night coming closer with their rein-chains and hooves making cold, unwelcome sounds in the moonwash. Lew took out his belt-gun and held it cocked, hanging low —waiting.

The first man reined up and gazed at the creek. He was an older man with hanging jowls and small eyes. He wore moccasins, baggy elk-skin britches and a greasy, shiny buckskin shirt. His shoulders sagged and his big, horny hands held the reins listlessly.

"Get down, brothers," he said. "We'll have a respite here."

There were seven of them, all glum and silent and forbidding looking. Lew breathed in short gulps and waited. He was almost sure—but not quite. Not yet.

15

The men dismounted. Their silhouettes were stiff-acting and weary. They had come a long way. The old fellow with the baggy pants knelt by the creek and washed his face and stared hypnotically at the water. He put both his hands in it and let it rinse over them. The other men drank deep and long; he didn't. His voice was husky but cracked and sluggish sounding.

"Not much farther now."

"Better not be," another voice said with pain laced through the words. "You know where it is, Henry?"

"I reckon," the old man said, looking off through the willows.

His action was enough. Lew's stomach bunched up slowly. The owl calls . . . the one that hadn't quite sounded true. He walked away from the black horse and hunkered, waiting.

"We ought t'see it pretty quick," another man said with a harshness. "It'll show up to-night."

"Maybe they didn't find it," the old man said. "God's Providence . . ." He let it trail off, looked at the water again, then, as though reminded of a duty forgotten, he bent low and drank.

Someone laughed with an ugly shortness. "They'll find it all right. They don't miss, them scum."

Lew's fists were damp and his nerves had raw ends that grated. He waited for the old man to speak again, after wiping his mouth on a sleeve. "They'll find it. Well, if we'd heard two hours earlier we'd a made them smart a mite." He looked off through the shielding willows again with tired old eyes. "May run across them over there or a-coming back. Bullard's a fighter; he'll keep 'em busy a spell. I knew him when he come here. He's—"

"Who are you, Mister?"

The men went rigid. They craned their necks, and only eyes showed in the brooding darkness. Eyes and the

16

weapons that were everywhere. The old man turned and studied Lew for a long moment before he answered, then his words came as though men with guns in their fists materialised out of all the nights of his old life.

"I'm Henry Mortonson—brother to Elder Jacob Mortonson. Does that mean anything to you, stranger?" The old eyes were neither frightened nor arrogant. They were just tired with a seeping weariness that wasn't of the flesh, but of the persecuted heart and suffering soul.

"Yes," Lew said. "I've heard Elder Mortonson speak." He looked at the others and hated what he had to say next. "I'm Lew Landsborough."

It came so quickly he could feel it. The wall of quick antagonism. He braced into it and returned their stares, acting as though he hadn't felt the freezing-up among them. "Where are you going?"

"To Zachary Bullard's place."

"Why?"

Henry Mortonson was on his knees, leaning back against his heels. He didn't move. "Because we got word the gentiles were night-riding."

"For Bullard's?"

Mortonson nodded and pushed tiredly up to his feet. He wasn't as tall as Lew, but he was broader, wider and as solid as a rugged old boulder. "Yes. Have you been there?"

"Just rode from there. We're kin."

"I know," Mortonson said, then his eyes dropped away and Lew felt the breath of guilt brush over him. He felt a need for cursing, but he didn't curse. The taint of him was over those whom he knew or had kinship with. He destroyed with his touch—his reputation—those whom he would have died to protect. It had happened before. He felt the fire of hot blood beating in under his cheeks, but the night was watery-dark.

Mortonson turned to his men. "Let's go on," he said, then he turned toward Lew with the same apathetic look. "You goin' on?"

Lew locked his teeth over a savage answer, waited, then spoke another word. "No. I'll lead you."

They mounted and waited until he got the black horse and swung out ahead of them. He watched the shapes of them straggling softly out of the willows. He reined back toward Mortonson.

"Can your horses stand a couple mile run?"

"Is that all we have to go?"

"No; but it'll put us over close enough to cut into them if they're coming back."

"No," Mortonson said slowly, thoughtfully. "We don't want to meet 'em on tucked-up horses. Jog if you want; we're good for a few miles o' that."

Lew did. He jogged with a big ball of fear and fury just behind his eyes. He was jogging far ahead of them when he saw it.

The symbol. The licking, sullen-angry firelight off on the horizon. He didn't turn to look back. Didn't care about the others. The black horse jumped out from the cruel, vicious raking of the spurs and went flat-eared and lunging-strided through the night.

Far behind old Henry Mortonson heard the drumroll of racing hooves and understood. His mouth lifted out of its terrible slackness and went inward a little. His face never changed expression and only the great welling up of pain that moved in the depth of his glance showed that he knew . . .

Once a man saw that red beacon, he could slow his horse. Nothing on God's earth could catch up in time, then. Always too late . . .

Lew felt the valiant animal stumble under him. He heard the shattered breath roaring, caught the grinding of the mightly muscles under him, and he had to slow down.

18

But he was close enough. Close enough—too close.

It resurrected a terrible anguish in him. Every fire he saw like that to the end of his life would always affect him the same way. Make him feel lost; sick with horror and weak with terror as though he were re-living something too overwhelmingly awful to survive. He left the horse without consciously doing it. He ran a quarter mile afoot, and there he stopped.

He was still standing there, a gaunt outline of a man growing old in the night, when the riders came ploddingly up, stopped and sat there with their faces made unreal, diabolical, in the flame-light. Hard, raw-boned faces with slitted eyes against the heat. Prominent jaws and cheek-bones limned terribly in the blood-glow of moving, twisting, flame.

Time swept by in the night and the riders fanned out in a peculiar silence. Spread out wide and used the fire-light to search for tracks. Then they came back to Mortonson and told him the gentile night-raiders had gone on up into the distant rain forest, and so were lost to vengeance. Then they waited—and waited. Lew felt himself emptied of grief so that he turned and saw the men behind him and threaded through them going back for his horse.

By dawn they could get close enough. There was the acrid stink in the air of charred flesh and death, and it was Mortonson himself who found Aunt Jem and Zack within six feet of one another. Zachary had fought a fierce battle. He was singed and wounded, and even after he was downed, his broad, mighty fingers had closed over the ground like talons and tore into its flinty earth. He was a hard man to kill. A fierce-stubborn man.

Lew knelt by Aunt Jem. The hands, the thin-veined hands with their power of soothing. He held them in his own palms for a while, then crossed them. Mortonson came up and glanced at him, started to say something and bit down hard. There was a wildness, a mania, almost, in the face of Lew Landsborough. A twisted, blasted, terrible look. Mortonson was stopped as though by a blow.

He turned and walked out a little way and knelt, a hulk of old man with steel-flake eyes full of a weariness of the soul. An old man tired to death of violence and bloodshed. A lover of peace and men and, mostly, of God. He knelt in his baggy old elk-skin britches with his Cheyenne moccasins; his greasy, ageless buckskin shirt—and he prayed :

"And—these things will they do unto you, because they have not known the Father, nor me."

Lew was still there between the dead when the old man came back and spoke.

"You'd better come to this other one."

Lew looked up into the grey-ghastly face. He got up slowly, like a man hard hit and unable to shake off the blow. Mortonson turned and led him. It was handsome Cal—like his mother in so many ways. The Elder stopped and waited for Lew to understand. The realisation came slowly, at first, then it burst over him with a staggering force. Insane!

Cal was burned. His hands were sickening to see, like raw red meat. Two powerful men stood over him with frightened, awed looks. They had marks from Cal on them. Bloody scratches and purpling bruises, and yet they showed no rancour, only a vast uneasiness in the face of something that was frightening. They had tied Cal, and in his dementia he was straining against the ropes like a great bull, so that his powerful back was arched under the stress. His eyes were darkly wild and open too wide. His lips were parted over strong white teeth and his corded neck was like a tree-trunk.

"Cal—don't."

Lew said it without effort. It had taken this to make him say anything, and all of a sudden the huge spiral of

20

grief within him collapsed and there was only the emptied feeling of loss, of ashes, in his mind. And pity, a painful, hurting pity for his cousin. Of them all . . .

"Are there—there was another son, Jay. Is he alive, too?"

Mortonson didn't look away from the straining madman. He shook his head. "Only this one. I don't know how he escaped bein' killed. God's mercy, I reckon."

"There was another one."

"I know. He's over by the barn. Must've been out there chorin' when they come. He caught it square in front up close. Never knew what hit him."

"Jay. They were my cousins."

"I know." Mortonson looked at the stalwarts over the bound man. "Salvage, boys. Planking for three boxes, if you can." He turned then and looked at Lew's profile. "Listen to me, Lewis Landsborough. If those gentiles knew you were visitin' these folks, then you've brought this on them."

The old man's steady, expressionless glance never wavered in the face of the towering wrath he faced suddenly. There was a dry, rasping bitterness in his voice. "I've heard o' you, and I say it's such men as you as have brought this upon us. This affliction. No, not altogether, but with your guns you've made the gentiles strike twice as hard. You took revenge before—I know your story—now you'll want it again. I saw that in your face, back yonder by the woman. Now listen to me. You can avenge these people. That's not the Lord's way—your own mother taught you that. But you can do it. Everyone knows you're a man with a deadly gun. And if you do you'll assure the deaths of others. Of our own people." Mortonson left it like that. He turned suddenly and walked away into the cold of the fresh new sunlight.

Lew stood perfectly still, with the choking fury like a

21

fire in his blood, watching the older man walk to where other men were dragging up old, half-rotten planks that hadn't burnt. He shook with his wrath while the flames licked gaspingly in fitful, sombre flickers over what was left.

Cal made some piteous, animal moans that distracted him. They were like icicles entering into his heart. He knelt and put a hand on the straining man. "Don't fight the ropes, Cal. Lie still."

Strangely, the dark-eyed man with his beet-red face all dappled with grimy sweat, went limp. His hair was matted and caked with dust, and saliva dampened the outer corners of his mouth like pale suds with a touch of dirt-brown to them. He locked his teeth with a grating sound and his dark eyes swept over Lew.

"Lie still, Cal." Beyond that there was nothing to say, so he said it again, and perhaps in repetition lay its magic, for the crazed man ceased to struggle altogether. "Lie still."

Mortonson came back. He was bareheaded, and the ugliness of his drab shock with its grey splatter made him an unpleasant image of a man. "Come on over. Come on over. We're ready."

They buried the Bullards, all but poor Caleb, in the un-relenting, bleak soil of their ranch yard, and Elder Morton-son proved himself an able man to pray. Lew stood there above the coarse mounds, seeing the sweat-stained armpits of the others. He heard the hard words fall flat and bleak in the sickly light, and such a fierceness surged through him that he was left weak after its passing.

Mortonson stopped. None spoke nor moved, and after a bit the old man raised his head with its deep fatigue, and looked squarely across the mounds at Lew. He said nothing. He didn't have to; and eloquence was in his eyes that he couldn't have worded anyway. They stood thus for perhaps a full minute, then Lew lifted his hat and dumped it on his head. He nodded to the others, shot old Mortonson a look just as eloquent as the one he'd received—and a hundred times as ruthless. He turned and went to his horse, only pausing when he saw the heart-searing look of Cal's glance as he passed. Then he bent swiftly and brushed the hair out of his cousin's face, and spoke.

"Cal? Can you hear me? Listen, Cal—I'll come back."

"Why?" The word thundered in a deep-rolling tone at him. He looked up swiftly and saw the patriarch standing there with his hair blowing and a strange fierceness in his cold eyes. "Why will you come back? For him? You needn't. We'll take him among us and give him prayer and comfort. All you'll ever do for him is bring back the terrors of this night. Don't come back, Lewis Landsborough —ever. Go far away and take the evil that's a blackness in your soul with you."

Lew spoke intently from where he knelt. "These were my kin. Those murdering gentiles have killed everyone I've ever loved. This—Cal here—this is what's left of my blood. Damn your mercy and meekness. Damn your forgiveness. Once, I might have . . . Twice, no man would. Four times—by God, no, Mortonson, that's more'n you'd do yourself. And this—this living death for Cal. No!" He stood up and the darkness was surging, pounding with a frightfulness within him so that it showed in his eyes.

"By God, no! If you think I was a scourge before— wait."

Mortonson's eyes held Lew's glance, but there was an agony of despair in them for a moment. A tortured anguish too deep and apparent to hide, then his iron fierceness came back. "You'll avenge no one, Landsborough. You'll only cause more of us to be killed."

"Get out, then. You're fools, anyway. Go to the rendezvous in the cane-brakes below St. Joseph. Go to Zion. They'll kill every last one of you, anyway."

"We're going. We're going. Because of you a lot of us'll never get there. Give us peace, Landsborough. We are sore beset on every side. Don't add to the suffering of your own kind, boy. Let us leave this land without more blood-letting."

Lew's mouth pulled inward against his teeth and a deadly glint showed in his face. "You've had no trigger-man up to the present, Mortonson. Now you have. You've got meekness and I've got something sounder—guns." He saw the deep disdain in the older man's glance again. The scorning contempt, almost hatred. "If you're going, then go; but I'll only wait until I'm sure who these men were. If that takes me a month, then you've got that much time." He turned swiftly and went toward his horse. Nor did he look back once, either.

Chapter Two

The sunlight came briefly, and after that there was a metal, sullen grey to the day. Gusty coughs of wind that soughed through the trees and made the old grass bow and twist. There wasn't a single redeeming feature to the day. The second and third days were the same, and then it got warm with a foreboding, an unhealthy warmth that filled things with an electricity of unrest and small fright.

Lew came out of the broken country near St. Joseph on that day. He saw the serpentine wagon-trains and the riders. The ox-teams with their oaken and hemlock neck-yokes. He saw the activity south where the dry land was powdery from much traffic, and he knew where the Mormon camp would be, from that. Northward a little, was the town. He sat the gaunt black horse with uncertainty. In the town he was fair game, an outlaw Mormon. In the camp of his people he was no better, for many thought as Zachary Bullard and Mortonson thought, that resistance had brought upon the persecuted the greater wrath of the gentiles. He reined for the town. At least his own people wouldn't betray him.

St. Joseph was trails-end. Beyond lay the primitive country; the Indians and the bulwark mountains. The swollen rivers and the path marked with stone cairns of the dead. St. Joseph, though, was something different. It was a town of men who lived off the migrating waves a-westering. People there were concerned with trade and profit more than ideologies. Still—the great hatred was there, too.

He rode in among the streams of riders. Wended his way around the wagons, the sluggish, incredible Conestogas. He saw the tide of empire all around him and heard its sounds in the ringing of anvils and the bawling of animals. Saw it in the weathered faces, the sunken eyes and the set-jaws of the people.

He found a place where he could buy feed for his horse. Stayed handy until he saw the animal eating well, then hiked through the everlasting bedlam for an old place, half mud, half logs, where he would find food. Inside, men were eating shoulder to shoulder at a scaffold-table. Venison, bear-meat, squash, butter-beans, cider and cheeses, and once there was a plum-pie, but it disappeared before it got near him. He ate, listening to the sounds of the rough wild place; looking into faces and seeing none he knew.

The hotel was an eating and sleeping place in one. There were filthy rolls of blankets and ticking tossed along the walls. There was a mighty, wide-open hearth made of sandstone slabs and hand-adzed timbers heavily packed over with clay. The walls were partly log with a moss-mud mixture pounded into the chinking against the congealing cold and winds that would come soon now.

He ate and paid and walked back outside. The air with its unhealthy warmth was thickening. He looked at the swollen old sky with its ragged wisps of darker grey at the fringes, and took some of its gloom for his own. Leaning against the wall, back from the burdened plankwalk, he watched people go by.

There was no pleasantness in any of their faces. Not even in the expressions of those who had security and a home nearby, for either men were desperate and lost in this brutal place, where a blacksmith might charge five dollars for shoeing an ox, or they were townsmen bent on squeezing out the last cent from a fleeing Mormon family—and secretly despising those Ishmaels of the frontier, too.

He waited several hours, then he watched the prairie gloaming come. A sick gloaming that partook of the malady of the sky's greyness. An evening of confused snarling in the town. It stifled him, so he got his horse and rode south, down toward the Mormon's rendezvous spot. Close enough, he could smell the cooking fires. Then, there were dark outlines of people, and wagons heaped crazily with hurried loads. Huge Conestogas, rope corrals, and bells ringing with different tones from oxen. Men and women and children. Then he was halted by a man sitting calmly on a rock with a rifle across his lap. The man seemed almost casual, there in the shadows, his new beard soft and downy and the rankness of his hair a mattress that broke out from the clamp of his flat-brimmed hat.

"Where you goin' stranger?"

"To the camp. You a guard?"

"I am. Who are you an' what you want down there?"

Lew looked down into the young face with the steady dark eyes. "I've got friends down there. I want to see them about going overland with 'em."

"Going where?"

"To Zion, friend," Lew said. "To Zion."

The guard ruminated, then tilted his head back a little. He made a soft smile. "You in a hurry, friend?"

"No, I reckon not; why?"

"Cussed lonesome out here," the guard said. "Everyone's in a hurry."

Lew dismounted and led his horse off the road and squatted in the gloom. "I understand lonesomeness," he said. "Even your kind that don't last long."

The guard bent a little farther forward, as though he were urging a horse to greater speed. The long rifle stayed behind his bent elbows across his upper legs. "You just come through St. Joe?"

"Yeah. Ate there."

"You feel the hate they got fer us, up there?"

Lew nodded. "Yes, it's there, but it don't amount to much. They're too busy taking our money and robbing for all they're worth."

"Yeh," the guard said. "An' we're strong, stranger. We got strength, now. Must be five hunnert folks yonder in the cane-brakes. Be a raw thing fer 'em if they come down here fer trouble."

"I reckon," Lew said dryly. "How long's this band been here?"

"It isn't one band. They keep stragglin' in every day. Come from everywhere. Illinois and Ohio and Missouri —from just about everywhere but out there." The guard bobbed his head toward the warm, night-shrouded plains across the Missouri river. "Too bad we don't get some from out there, too. It'll be hard, makin' out, I reckon."

Lew looked into the west. There was nothing to see; just the deep-throatiness of the river hurrying on to its destiny. Rushing and eddying and cresting with oily waves; blind to everything but its own destiny. He listened to it and heard the subtle change.

Somewhere, a long way north of them perhaps, the warmth in the air, that great swollen bladder of sky, had burst. The water was rising; warning with its murmur.

He got up and ran the reins through his fingers and looked down the land where the ominousness of the sultry night was stabbed again and again by thin daggers of fire-light. The lowering gut of the heavens was inflamed with the myriad cooking fires, and angry little sparks showed against it. The smell was good. He saw frightened bats, confused and lost in the stillness, plummet erratically through the air, barely overhead, then he looked at the youth with the proud new beard again.

"When'll they commence crossing?"

"Soon, I reckon. Some're waitin' for Elder Mortonson. Word has it he's coming. Some won't wait. My outfit'll push off maybe three, four days. When you leavin'?"

"Oh, it don't make much difference for a man alone and astride. Anyway, I don't know. I have to talk to my friends. Well," he turned and mounted with a slow smile, "I don't envy you that chore."

The guard laughed. "It's wearisome and useless, but camp law is camp law."

Lew rode on down among the scattered, erratic camps. It was like a huge band of Indians. There were dogs and dog-fights and men threading their ways in silence through the night. Faces turned up quickly to see a horseman go past, then averted with a harassed glance for the gusty fires and the black iron pots that hung over them.

He saw the entire panoply of suffering people wrenched up by the roots and cast out from their homes, huddled beside the muddy, threatening river. The anger lay in him like a dormant fire, banked beyond the depth of despair and loss he felt in the very air he breathed and rode through.

A man with a blanket around his shoulders stood up as he passed and watched him, turning, turning, peering into his face, turning to follow his passage as though drawn by a magnetic load. Lew saw and wondered, hesitated, then went back and sat calmly above the man's face, looking into it. He knew him.

"Evening, Crawford." There was no warmth in the greeting, simply acknowledgment. The man called Crawford had muddy-coloured eyes and skin to match. He was angular and awkward-looking, with cowhide boots worn and scuffed, and a pistol girded to his middle. He spoke with a voice oddly out of place in such a body. A shrill, nasal rasp that was Missouri through and through.

"Ye're goin' too, I see."

Lew considered the man. Charley Crawford had come out of the eastern country. He had been in the valley when Lew's tragedy had come. He had been one of those who spoke out the loudest against Lew's reprisals—and here he was, fleeing like the others.

"I'm goin'," Lew said. "They killed the Bullards."

"I heard," Crawford said. His voice was half-antagonistic, half-subdued. "They kilt 'em a'ter you was there."

Lew's temper rattled like a sabre loose in the scabbard. He waited a second, then spoke again. "They were out there in the night already. It wouldn't have mattered. That's what I tried to say while I was there. Night-riders were goin' farther afield, Crawford. You know that. If you didn't, you wouldn't be here, now."

Crawford looked away. The glow of a cooking fire caught his dirty-looking face and glanced off it, coppery-quick. "It don't matter now. Just gettin' across that—" Crawford swung one arm and pointed with it, rigidly, out into the night.

Lew understood. There was a fear in them all, evidently, about the route ahead. The overland country that would bring them to Zion. He wondered at this fear. After what they were escaping, what terror could rivers and mountains and Indians hold for them?

"I'd rather take my chances there than here, Crawford."

"I reckon ye would," Crawford shot back with a quick lifting of his face. "Was I wearin' ye're boots, I'd rather, too."

Lew was drawn off by the approach of another man. Younger, larger, and broader than Crawford. He returned the man's nod and ignored his inquiring look. Crawford would say it—Lew wouldn't have to. Crawford did, half

30

turning to the newcomer with his muddy eyes dour and his mouth thin.

"That's Lew Landsborough."

The other man's glance came back slower. It ranged over Lew and the black horse with complete impassibility. The man was quiet for a spell, then he looked Lew squarely in the face. "Get down. Have you eaten?"

"Yes," Lew said, making no move to dismount, "I've eaten, thanks."

"Then get down and come on over where there's a council. We'd like to talk to you."

"I doubt it," Lew said dryly. "You might; the others wouldn't."

"I'll vouch for them. Get down."

Lew dismounted and stood beside his horse threading the reins through his fingers. The man was larger afoot than he'd looked ahorseback. Lew considered him. Maybe thirty, maybe twenty-five. He had an open face and fearless eyes and no beard. He wore his gun like it belonged around his middle, and his legs were wide and mighty-looking. "Who're you?"

"Danton Mills. Leave your horse here at Crawford's camp."

They went, the three of them, Crawford hurrying ahead for a purpose that Lew never doubted, and Danton Mills striding through the confusion beside Lew.

"I've heard a lot about you."

"I reckon," Lew said dryly. "Ever hear anything good?"

Mills chuckled. It was a deep, pleasant sound. "Not much," he admitted. "But we all don't think alike, either."

"Meaning what?"

"That I don't believe in forever turning the other cheek or always running."

Lew looked at Mills and understood that he'd feel that way, as powerful and strong as he was. "You'll find out we're a minority as soon's I squat around your fire, though."

31

"No," Mills said slowly. "This here is different from back home. Here, you've got people deep in suffering. A lot of 'em are stubborn. A lot ain't. There's men'll fight now that wouldn't 'a fought before. You'll see."

Lew strode into the glow and warmth of the fire and saw at once that Crawford had done his job well. He was met with impassive faces and flickering stares. He felt the silence as though it were a tangible barrier between him and those men, but he squatted anyway, with his knack of patient waiting—and waited.

Danton Mills did the talking. His voice was a little like Jakob Mortonson's voice. Deep and like rolling thunder with an echo both strong and sombre. He heard the words without listening. Defiant words that hammered home the need for strength among the people. Words that lashed the council with their appeal for strength. And lastly, challenging words that defied any of them there this night to shy away from one of them who had seen his own blood poured out over their old land and who had struck back fiercely in retaliation.

He looked from beneath his hatbrim at the faces. There was outrage in some, wonder in others, a resolute stoniness in others. It was impossible to say what thoughts lay in those shaggy heads. He waited. Mills turned swiftly and motioned for Lew to rise. He did it slowly, suddenly conscious of the type of weariness that old Mortonson had in his fibres. Not weariness of the body, but a deeper, more draining kind. A weariness, almost a sickness, of the soul.

"You're among us as one of us. We need you, Landsborough. I think we all want you with us. You've seen a lot lately—tell them." Mills sat down on the ground and looked at the fire-lit faces with a cold glance that flared out at them all.

Lew stood loose-limbed, feeling the futility of speaking to those faces. They weren't men, just hunched-up bodies with dull red faces looking at him. Anyway, there was nothing he could tell them he hadn't told others like them a hundred times before, and had it rejected.

"Well, I reckon I'm known to some of you. I don't suppose I'm liked by many. I'm goin' to Zion." He was aware of a lack of purpose in his words and strove to rally his thoughts. It wasn't much of a success, that rallying; not with those hard faces looking up with no encouragement in them. He spoke on, holding the edges of his mind by force alone, so that his voice was a drone. A thing that revealed nothing of its owner.

"I'll make one suggestion to you; you can take it or leave. Break your camps right now and get across that river."

There was a prolonged silence, then a squat, broad man with slighting protruding eyes spoke up. "Why? Raiders coming from that town?" He said it as though the town were something physical. Something to be despised, like a man.

"No, it isn't that. Or, if it is, I don't know anything about it. But the river's rising. I heard it back a ways. It's probably going to flood to-night. Maybe a cloudburst back in the mountains—I don't know."

Danton Mills was staring sombrely into the fire. "How about the ferry? They won't haul us to-night, will they?"

Lew felt irritation. "They'll haul you if you make it worth their while. Like everything else in St. Joseph; there's a price. Anyway, what I'm saying is get across to-night. To-morrow may be too late, and if it is, you'll be camping here a week from now." He shrugged. "If you've got money to pay for St. Joseph's food, then you're all right to stay. I don't think you have, though."

The ring of faces dropped away a little, a few at a time. The men seemed to be considering this new threat. Lew could see their shoulders sag a little. He should have felt pity for them, but he didn't. He turned and started to walk away. A man called out to him. It was an unfamiliar voice; a deep, ringing voice with a hardness to it.

"Wait a minute. Hold up."

Lew turned and waited. The man was rising. He was stiff, either with hard-used muscles or age; it was hard to tell when his head was averted. But he was a stalwart man, well put together. Then he turned his head, and Lew wondered that he hadn't recognised the voice before. Elder Mortonson. The guard out along the roadway had said they were waiting for him. He must have taken a horse and ridden ahead of his wagons.

"We aren't here to judge you, or any man. We are a race beset with travail. Those of us who will help, are welcome." The big man paused. He was speaking softly, watching Lew's face without blinking. "Will you go tell the ferryman we're coming?"

"Yes," Lew answered quietly, seeing Danton Mills arise from his place. "He'll set a price."

"We'll pay it. You're right; we've got to be across by sunup. There's a smell of rain in the air."

Lew walked to his horse and turned only when he was in the saddle. Mills was looking up at him. "Wait a minute and I'll ride with you."

Lew waited, watching Crawford come back to his camp with his face averted. A longing to drop some of his acid on the man was strong. He refrained. Crawford wasn't worth it.

He saw Mills' shadow and reined off without waiting. When the larger man caught up, they rode in silence down along the riverbank, thence up toward the town. Closer, the incessant clamour of the place came to them. Mills pointed toward a shack and a looming shapelessness that rode with clumsy and uneasy grace, the swift-running water.

"It's over there."

Lew said nothing. They rode closer, until the rotting smells of water's-edge were thick, then they left their horses and walked down a swaying planking of sorts to a shack. Lamp light came out and splashed on them. Lew knuckled the door and stood back, waiting. A man came out and peered scowlingly at them. He looked twice at Danton Mills.

"What'll ye have, boys?"

"Passage across, mister."

The beetling brows came inward and downward swiftly. "In the mornin'. What's the hurry?"

Lew moved a little closer. Crossing now—to-night—for the Mormon wagons and rigs."

"That crew?" the man said, both surprised and antagonised. "Damn, it'd take all night. 'Sides, it's fixin' t'storm. Let 'em—"

"How much a head for men and critters?"

The disgruntled look took on an annoyance at Lew's quiet persistence. The man's temple-vein throbbed, but he studied them both for a long time before he spoke again. "Dollar a head, an' I say let 'em wait."

Lew edged still closer. The lamp light over the man's shoulder fell across one side of his face. One eye glowed steadily, without warmth. "Dollar a wagon; dime for loose-stock. And now—to-night." The ferryman swore mightily. Lew was unperturbed. "There's a lot of strong arms among them. They'll do the pulling themselves. You'll have no work to do. We're going back to get 'em rolling. You be ready."

The ferryman fell into a hard silence. He watched them both turn and walk toward their horses. The lean one was a deadly acting cuss. Never raised his voice; probably a damned Mormon renegade. And the big one . . . The ferryman spat into the lapping water and cursed with a

35

knack for vividness that goes with men who live along disagreeable rivers.

Mormons! . . . Damned Mormons! . . .

Elder Mortonson was standing out in the path when they
came back. He said nothing, nor moved out of their way
so that they had to rein up. He ignored Danton Mills.
"Well?"

"Dollar a person and a dime per head for stock."

Mortonson, a powerful wedge of man from thick
shoulders to lean hips, made a savage sound in his throat
that would have been terrible profanity in any other man.
He clenched his big fists. "It's robbery."

Lew nodded, watching the play of dark blood mantling
into the patriarch's face, and out again, as he fought with
his anger. "I reckon it is, and if it doesn't rain an' flood
that river, you'll hate me worse'n you ever did."

Mortonson relaxed a little, looking at Lew. "I hate no
man," he said, and the very way he said it gave it the lie.
A deep, rumbling blast of a thundering voice set in denial.

Lew smiled crookedly, giving stare for stare. "I don't
believe you," he said softly. Danton Mills winced. Lew's
little wry smile remained, a haunting look in the warm
darkness. "But I'm no more concerned than you are. Get
'em rolling, Elder. St. Joseph is pretty quiet now. Maybe
we can get 'em through the road and across the river before
we waken the place. Be best that way."

Mortonson's big features were moulded into a look of
coldness. "I'm not often called a liar," he said.

Lew gathered his reins. "Later, maybe. Right now let's
cross the muddy Missouri."

And they did. The great surging mass of men and women
and children. A tide of wagons and Red River carts. Dogs
and drovers' whips cracking with a pistol-sound. Men
walking over the hard earth in flat boots goading their
oxen. Faster moving vehicles with spans of horses. Latter
Day Saints leaving the known for the unknown, and the

River Jordan was the Missouri. Big and broad; making sucking, hungry sounds, cresting more and more with dark objects swirling by. The ferryman watched them come with rancour in his face. Anxiety too, for if he held them up they would back up and overflow into St. Joseph, and there'd be plenty of men who'd blame him for a thing like that. Damned—doubly damned—Mormons!

Lew leaned down from his saddle with a mocking, sardonic look. "Place 'em, mister. You know how to load that barge."

The ferryman swore again. As well try to order off the clouds or the rain or the prairie winds as turn them back now. He motioned for the first huge Conestogas to come on. He swung toward Lew with an angry squint. "Send up the men as'll pull 'er across."

They went, Lew sitting to one side watching; listening to the lowing of uneasy oxen and the quick, sharp nickering of horses. He could see the straining faces of the men and the anxious look of the women. And there were children peering excitedly from under canvas wagon-shrouds and old ticking-mattresses and quilts tied with black yarn.

He turned and studied the great snake of dispossessed people. They swung down from the ferry landing and over into the town. There were lights now where there had been none before. St. Joseph was turning out to watch the pariahs cross from civilisation to the vague pastures called "the frontier". He knew with a sore heart how those at the end of the line would endure the insults of the townsmen and the taunts. He knew also, that back there were many strong men—there would be no trouble.

"'Nother train just come up."

He turned and looked into the large features of Danton Mills. The man rode a powerful chestnut horse. His shock of disarrayed hair was clamped under a low-crowned hat and his blue eyes were alive so that they shone in the sickly light.

"Are they in the line?"

"Wheelin' in now; it was Mortonson's people. They and some others they picked up on the way." Mills eyed him thoughtfully. "You see—I was about right. They listened to you."

Lew smiled without mirth. "I reckon. After they smelt the rain in the air. No matter."

Mills looked over where a group of horsemen were congregating. In their midst, a towering figure, was Elder Mortonson. He reined away from Lew, wound his way through the line of wagons and animals and men. Lew watched him go, then turned his black horse and rode down the line. Only a few recognised him, and one of them was Crawford.

"Hey! What's the hold-up?"

Lew reined on by without answering. Rode all the way back to the end of the line and saw the loitering men back there in the town. Some were full of ribald, cutting humour. Others were silent and stony-faced. He rode along the new wagons and saw men congregating near a horseman who was sitting erect, ignoring them, beside an old wagon. They cat-called, none of it gentle and a lot of it dangerously close to fight-talk. He watched the rider as he rode slowly closer.

A man stepped down off the plankwalk—a big man, burly and fierce looking. He crossed to the horseman and stopped with his hands on his hips, too close. Lew couldn't hear what he said, but he recognised the imminence of an explosion and took down his lariat with a quick twist; then, before he shook out the little catch-loop, the rider appeared to lean sideways a little. Something whistled through the air with a solid dullness. The man staggered and almost went down. His hands were over his face; he swore a vicious curse and looked out of the fingers turning crimson. Quirted. It went through Lew's mind with no particular satisfaction.

He kept his horse walking. The man afoot had lost his hat. He was wild looking. Lew tossed. The noose settled nicely around the man's shoulders. A spin and a flat-footed walk back up the row of wagons was enough.

He sat twisted in the saddle, watching. It had happened fast. The bystanders were still undetermined and the man at the end of the rope bounced and dragged and let out a big cry. Lew heard men and looked ahead. He recognised Danton Mills and Elder Mortonson among the clutch of hard-faced men riding past him. None of them appeared to see him until they were close to the straining man at the end of his rope; then the Elder got down ponderously, circled his horse, lifted the burly man to his feet with one arm and pulled Lew's rope off.

The man's face was a shambles. What the quirt hadn't torn the ground had. He was scratched and gouged, but his eyes blazed with an intent, savage light. Lew sat, watching.

"You goddamned Mormons," the man said. "I'll kill you for this."

Danton Mills leaned out of his saddle. "Better fetch lots of balls," he said; "there's a heap of us to kill."

Elder Mortonson dropped his hand from the man's arm. There was a cold look to his face. "I'm sorry, friend. Your pain isn't a tenth of what ours has been."

The bystanders were moving by then. Danton Mills looked at them from beneath craggy brows. "Settle down, friends. Settle down." It worked on a lot of them; some called back but most of them confined their animus to ugly looks. There were at least thirty Mormon horsemen there, beside that wagon.

The injured man went back to his friends. Elder Mortonson turned slowly. Lew could feel the wrath of his look in the silence and the gloom. He took it with the only weapon he had against abuse of that kind—patience.

Mortonson turned away from him finally, led his horse over beside the quirt-bearing rider, handed up his reins and swung up onto the high seat of the wagon beside the grizzled driver. They looked a lot alike, someway. Lew watched them until Danton Mills rode over beside him and spoke in a low voice.

"I'm glad you did it like that."

"Are you?" Lew said dryly. "The Elder isn't."

"A bullet'd of started a war with 'em, the scum. The filthy border scum."

Lew watched the wagons move up a little. Mills spoke softly, mockingly. "Across the River Jordan," he said.

"Or," Lew said, "the River Styx."

Mills regarded Lew's profile guardedly. It was a lean, clearly defined profile that had strength and a measure of poignancy to it. A face with a strange stillness around the mouth and an unmoving alertness around the eyes. A hunted man's face.

He watched the wagons move sluggishly and looked at the sky. "Be dawn directly," he said conversationally. Lew reined away from him and rode back up the line, coiling his lariat as he went. Mills was a nice fellow; trouble was he hadn't lived in the depths of loneliness enough to know that you don't have to keep up a running conversation to be in another man's company.

He went all the way back to the ferry and watched the men load it. There was a fierceness to their struggles with frightened, balking animals and too-heavy wagons, but only the ferryman swore—he who was doing the least work; scuttling among the Mormons collecting his passage fees.

The remainder of the ragged night passed that way. By daylight, when the river-mists, dirty, brownish, odorous, were abroad, the line was shrunken to a little queue on the St. Joseph side, and when the last wagon went grinding over the cleated, shredded decking of the barge, Lew followed it. He was the last of the Mormons to leave the settled and known parts of the land.

He dismounted and stood beside his black horse, watching the land fall away; feeling the great surging, the insistent hurrying of the mighty tide of the Missouri. The depth of loneliness in him grew and filled his being. Forever and ever . . .

They were all back there somewhere. Even poor Caleb. There was a way of knowing, too. He would never visit them again. Never. Their graves would be left for others to wonder at; for the deep-brooding rain forests to look down upon, heavy and mysterious, frighteningly solemn and dark, stretching farther than anyone knew. The thick leaves and needles whispering and closing out the sun. He would never return.

"Mister Landsborough?"

He turned. Instant surprise jarred him, but it didn't show. A woman—a girl, really. Pretty and tired looking, with blue shadows under bluer eyes. A vague stirring moved within him, but he didn't try to hold it, and it died away. Only the liquid hurt still showed in his eyes. "Yes'm."

"Thank you for handling that man, back there."

"The man? Oh, were you in that wagon?"

"No. I was the one on the horse beside it."

He considered that, wonderingly. The rider had been astride. Women didn't ride astride; it wasn't decent— wasn't lady-like. Things were all topsy-turvy now, though. It could have been her.

"It wasn't anything." He wanted to turn back. There was a sense of urgency in him to look once more at the settled land.

"Well—" she sounded tart. He looked swiftly back to her.

"I'm sorry, ma'm." He motioned toward the land and

the lights of St. Joseph, Missouri. "That's the world, back there."

She looked at it with no apparent liking. "That's only another unpleasant episode. We're going to Zion." The last four words had a suppressed thrill in them. He could feel their tug of excitement. He looked at her face, then back to the orange dots of lamp light.

"Unpleasant episode," he echoed her. "Maybe. I've left kinsmen back there."

"So have I," she said.

"Dead?"

She looked away from his face swiftly. "No; not dead."

He didn't say what he was thinking; instead he looked down when a great grinding noise grated from the bowels of the old barge, made it slew a little off the course. "Light enough to see now." He spoke absently, as though to his horse. "I think I was right."

"What do you mean?"

He looked back at her. She was very pretty. Like a prairie flower that shone more alluring as the light brightened in a new day. "I figured last night the river would flood. That there was heavy rain up north somewhere. That it'd come down here and make crossing impossible. I got your Elder Mortonson to cross 'em all last night." He made a wan smile. "Glad I was right. Would've been sort of embarrassing if I'd been wrong."

"And expensive," she said, with that tartness to her voice again. "Well, thank you, Mister Landsborough. I'm in your debt."

"You're plumb welcome. No, you don't owe me a thing."

She turned without smiling and went back forward, weaving her way past people and animals and vehicles. Lew watched her until she was out of sight, then glanced up and saw the faces turned his way. Not until then did he feel acute discomfort; not until then did he look swiftly

42

out over the broad river in order to avoid the stares, and curse under his breath, tightening his grip on the reins.

They landed, and again Lew was the last man to touch the heavy ground. He led his horse out of the jumble of men and equipment, mounted up and rode off a little way. Four men came toward him. He saw them and knew they were riding after him. He reined up, waiting. When they were close enough he recognised Elder Mortonson, Danton Mills, and—of all things—Jakob Mortonson, still in his baggy elk-skin britches. The fourth rider was the girl. She was astride. He looked away, then back again. She rode well; was well formed. He looked away again and waited.

When they were close enough they reined up. Elder Mortonson regarded him woodenly. "You've served us well. We all thank you."

Lew's eyes puckered a little. "But—you'd like me to travel on. That it?"

Jakob spoke next. He still had his disapproval like a torch, in his face. "You did my daughter a turn last night. I thank you for her." Lew looked his swift surprise at the girl. She was looking at him very closely, unblinking. He thought he saw something besides wonder in her look, but couldn't place it. He shrugged.

"Like I told her. It was nothing."

Jakob went on in his rumbling voice. "Well, you didn't go after the killers of your aunt and uncle, and we thank you for that, too. It gave us the time to get away."

Elder Mortonson spoke next. Harshly, as though wanting to terminate an unpleasant duty. "Lewis? Will you forego your vengeance?"

"Why should I?"

"Because we'd like to have you ride with us to Zion. We need able men. The way is long and hard. Our troubles haven't begun yet. Listen to me; what's behind is behind. The Lord will take vengeance. It's neither your right nor your privilege. Turn away, Lewis Landsborough.

43

Turn away from your pain and hatred and come into the fold of your mother's and father's people. Turn your back on the past, son. Ride with us to Zion and share the fruits of all our labours. On this side of the river you are a Mormon; a fellow, a brother to us all." Mortonson swung an arm backwards dramatically, without looking away from Lew's face. "Back there is more sin and iniquity for you. Onward, there is a new life waiting."

Lew listened. His glance wavered; it went from face to face, then settled on Jakob Mortonson's craggy features. There was a cold depth of hardness in the glance. "Where's my cousin?"

The girl spoke ahead of her father. "In our wagon. He's—he's—"

"I know," Lew said softly, still looking at Jakob. "You know what my answer is. Listen, I came here for two purposes. I've seen one of 'em accomplished. You-all are on your way now. The other is to see what I can hear, before I head back. There are men in this place who'll know who those night-riders are."

"I doubt it," Danton Mills said.

"If there aren't, I'll go back—but I'll find them. I told you back there, at the Bullard place; I've taken more than one man's share. Five dead—one insane—I want to settle with them, and I will!"

The three men sat in stony-eyed silence. Only the girl didn't seem to understand the wall of growing stubbornness that was all around them. She looked past her father and uncle, and Danton Mills.

"You're wrong, Mister Landsborough. Your cousin isn't insane. Ride back with me; let me show you."

44

Chapter Three

He went back with her. All the way through the jumbled
mess of the camp arighting itself and setting up breakfast
cooking fires. Beyond most of the wagons to where the last
barge-load had disembarked. She stopped near a grey,
worn wagon, swung down and looped her reins around a
forward wheel. He did, too, then he walked behind her
to where a familiar bulk of man was bent low over
whittlings, coaxing a little fire to life.

"Cal?" She stopped beside the hunched over man. Lew
couldn't see his face. Only the ragged blanket across his
great shoulders and the floppy hat. He came off his haunches
slowly, stood up and towered over her. Lew was back
a ways. He saw the dark, soft eyes—Aunt Jem's eyes—
fasten to her face. He went closer, unable to tear his gaze
from his cousin's face. The girl's voice was soft and caress-
ing. "Do you remember the man I was talking to you about
last night? Your cousin?"

"Yes'm," Cal said slowly. "Lew. I remember him."

"He's here."

The dark eyes had a swiftly passing cloudiness to them.
"Here?"

Lew was close enough when he spoke. "Here, Cal."

The heavy, massive man raised his head a little and
looked past the girl. Their eyes held, his and Lew's. A

45

quick flash of agitation showed in the dark eyes. Bullard's mouth worked a little, as though whispering, and Lew's heart was squeezed by a mighty and relentless fist.

"Cal, I'm glad for you. Mighty glad for you." He held out his hand. The other man regarded it solemnly and didn't take it. Lew let it fall to his side. The old hurt came back; the old thought with its acid painfulness. Those he touched, he destroyed. The invisible thread of kinship was broken.

"Wait."

He turned back, seeing the strange way she was looking at him. "Well?" He said it patiently.

She had one hand on Cal's arm. He could see where the fingers were indenting the sleeve from her tight grip, then she swung abruptly to Cal and smiled up into his face—the scarred face where burn-scars were pink and ugly. "I'll be back in a bit, Cal."

Lew fell in beside her after one swift glance at Caleb. The broad back was bending over the little fire again, oblivious to all else. They walked past people whose covert glances he felt and ignored them with annoyance. Back near where his horse stood, she spoke again.

"You didn't expect to see him like that, did you? I mean, rational and all, did you?"

He looked at the ground when he answered. "I don't know exactly what I expected to see. He's favouring though, isn't he?"

"He's recovering well," she said, watching his face closely. "It's been a nightmare for him. He—well—he isn't at all like you."

Lew shrugged thoughtfully. "He isn't like any of them, except his mother, my Aunt Jem. His brother was rock-hard. So was his father. I never understood it, exactly. He's got the strength of two men—all the Bullard men had it—but there's a lot of his mother in him. Always has been." He looked up quickly, wondering if he sounded mawkish. "I'm beholden to you, lady, for what you've done with him."

"Are you?" she said quickly, eyes shining with intentness. "Then do your share for him, too."

"What do you mean?"

"Didn't you notice the haunted look he got, for a second, when he saw you?"

"Yes'm. I'm nothing he wants to remember, I reckon."

"But he has to. He's got to face it all in due time. Learn to master every bit of the agitation that overcomes him from time to time. If he doesn't, he'll never be fully recovered."

"Well—I know nothing of such things," he said lamely.

She spoke swiftly, with hard force now. "You said you were beholden to me. Then pay that debt and the debt of blood to him by staying with us. Going on to Zion with us. Getting to know him again. Help him; he's the last of your kin, my father told me. You owe him that."

She had a fierce intensity to her. Almost a breathlessness. It rolled up against his blind-stubborn resolve like a mighty floodwater. She was standing erect, almost rigid, and staring into his face wide-eyed.

"For his sake and your own. He's alive; those others are dead. You can't help the dead, but you *can* help the living."

He looked into her face, saw the drive, the forcefulness, the shattering steadiness of her eyes the way they looked into him—past him and through him almost—and had a stirring of strangeness. She had a way of looking at a person as though she was . . .

He dropped his glance quickly to her hands. Hands that showed with their small gestures that there was a power of strength in them. Aunt Jem's hands. It frightened him a little. He looked up into her face again.

"Tell me something, ma'm. Did he commence getting

47

better as soon as you started taking care of him?"

She looked away from him uneasily and answered with her head averted. "Yes, as soon as my father brought him home tied with ropes and I took the ropes off."

He followed her line of vision, and saw the distant spiral of smoke and the hunched over figure with the sloppy old blanket and dirty old hat. "I'll stay, ma'm," he said. "I'll go on to Zion with you. I figured to all the time, but—"

"But you wanted to make one trip back first."

"Yes; they'll go unavenged."

"No, they won't. 'Vengeance is mine, saith the Lord.'"

He let his glance swing out over the great sprawling camp, down to the river and across it, where squalor was in buildings, and St. Joseph lay. He could see the ferryman loading horsemen aboard his barge. It looked like a big party. More Saints, probably . . .

"I'm very glad." She said it simply, and drew his attention back to her with the softness of the words. He watched her walking back toward the old Mortonson wagon. Was still standing there with his thoughts when Danton Mills and Charley Crawford came up and spoke to him.

"Elder Mortonson wants to see ye, Lew."

He felt distaste for Crawford. It showed in his face. He looked inc liringly at Mills, got an exaggerated shrug of the big shoulders, fell in with them and walked to where men were congregated in a careless circle.

The air had lost its warmth. There was a snaking wind that wound among the vehicles, making sad sounds and flapping tag-ends of canvas and quilting. He studied the great mass of scudding filth that was the dirty sky. It wouldn't be long now before they'd all get wet. One of the men in the group around the leader was leaning on his big wooden shovel, with its plank spade-part edged with hammered iron. He was freckled, sturdy, and worried-looking.

Lew stopped and caught their stares, waiting. The Elder spoke without preliminaries.

"When you roped that man and dragged him last night, the men of St. Joseph guessed who you were."

Lew waited. He knew what must be said now, for he had used the identical means of hauling three men out of their dooryards years back. Dragging them like logs until he'd shot them. The marauders who'd killed his parents. It had been a terrible thing to do. A grisly thing, and the doing had horrified a lot of people—they had remembered. The whole frontier remembered. He thought dourly that any man who roped and dragged another man was likely to be lynched as the Mormon renegade, Lewis Landsborough.

"I'll go away," he said simply.

The man leaning on the wooden shovel wore an old black sweater with a very soiled vest over it. He evidently had been working at the edge of the river, for there was river mud on his trousers. He shook his head slowly from side to side. "It'll do ye no good now," he said. "They're coming."

And they were. A band of riders coming slowly from the landing. Perhaps thirty of them, all armed to the teeth, hard-looking men, ugly and formidable. Outnumbered but sure in their strength, for they had a man of law with them. He rode ahead with the badge of office on his woollen coat.

Lew watched them riding toward the little group. He saw Charley Crawford's adam's apple bob frantically twice. He saw Danton Mills' big face, with its open frankness, congeal into a stubborn coldness and guessed the big man must have always looked like this when gentiles came close to him with their hatred and their guns. He turned and looked squarely at Elder Mortonson. Behind him a little was Mortonson's brother, with the sick-tiredness in his face.

"I'll go with them," he said.

Elder Mortonson didn't answer. He didn't even look at Lew. The horsemen were close enough to rein up, sitting their saddles like wooden chips hacked clumsily into the shapes of men.

"You the leader o' these folk?" The lawman was a sparse, wisp-haired, faded-looking man with bitterness in his eyes. His voice was a weak, shrill sound in the lowering storminess. Elder Mortonson answered with a voice more appropriate. He thundered his answer without any softness to it.

"I am. Who are you?"

"I'm the United States Marshal. Name's Mueller—if that's anything to you."

"What do you want here?"

Mueller's eyes flicked over the group, rested on Lew for a moment, then went back to Mortonson's face. "That man," he said.

"Why?"

"Why?" the marshal said rapidly. "Because he's a damned outlaw."

"Curb your tongue," Danton Mills said angrily.

Elder Mortonson shot Mills a glance then looked back at the man on the horse. "How do you know this man's an outlaw?"

The lawman's face was colouring with a russet hue. His eyes were getting stormy. "There are men in St. Joe who've seen him. They know him to be L. M. Landsborough, Mormon renegade wanted by the law for murder."

"Show me one man," Elder Mortonson said, "who can identify this man, and I'll hand him over to you."

The marshal swung a little in his saddle. "Gerrit—come up here."

The man came. Lew recognised him in the daylight only because of his hefty build and the wreckage of his face. The quirt mark was purple, badly swollen and livid-looking. The other marks were almost as bad. The man's little

50

eyes showed balefully. He had the inner illness of most bullies; the sickness of victory without personal triumph. Lew stepped out casually before the mounted men.

"You mean this man'll identify me for an outlaw?"

The marshal nodded. "Speak out, Gerrit."

Lew laughed. It was a hard, rasping sound. "He got manhandled; that scum. Now he'll say I'm anybody and you'll take his word for it. I never saw that man before last night, in my life, and he never saw me."

Gerrit's angry look shifted often. The marshal was getting angrier. "Damn it all, Gerrit; identify him!"

"Sure. That there's Landsborough. I seen him back in Kelso County and again over in Brazo Valley."

A deepening silence fell over the men. Lew stood in the middle of it looking up at Gerrit with a strange, milky cast to his glance. He was rigid with an awful awakening. Slowly, he looked past the horsemen to the tree-fringed edge of the river. The stark limbs stood out sharp, cold, dark against the paleness of the sky with its greying threat.

"Where did you see me in Brazo Valley?"

Gerrit spoke stronger now. "At Bullard's one night."

The odd look Gerrit got wasn't wrathful. It was a cold, deadly look. "The night the Bullards were killed. That was the only night I'd been in that yard in fifteen months. It *was* that night, wasn't it?"

"Yeh." Gerrit looked at his companions. Most of them were watching Lew in fascination. They didn't even see the girl come up on the fringe of the circle. The girl and the squat, mighty man with the grey old blanket clutched tightly around his shoulders and a flickering agitation in his dark, liquid eyes. "It was the night Bullard's got burnt out. On'y none o' us knew who you was until a'ter you'd rode off. Some went a'ter you, but they run inter a flock of damned Mormons a-comin'. You was goddamned lucky that night."

Lew turned away from Gerrit. He caught a ragged flash

of an importuning glance from the girl and swung farther. He saw Jakob Mortonson beside his brother. They had been talking. Lew knew what about. He gestured with one hand. "A gentile night-rider. Ask your brother what my kinsmen looked like when he got there. Ask him if they had a chance at all. I will go with them if you say."

Elder Mortonson's eyes were troubled. He said nothing. More and more men came up. They carried arms of all kinds, even bare knives and old cavalry sabres, wicked and curved and dull-shining in the grey light.

The possemen were losing some of their aplomb.

Lew caught the girl's glance. It was as though his gaze was snagged by it, like a buck-thorn sticker. He couldn't read anything in it. Caleb was clutching his blanket and his big hands were white-knuckled. A shaft of deep pity hit Lew. He had a responsibility for Cal. He turned back toward the riders as the first wind-driven drizzle lashed them all and the sound of the river became increasingly ominous with its growing panic of muddy hurry.

"Marshal, you're across the Missouri. Your right to take a man here isn't lawful, it seems to me."

"What the hell're you talkin' about, Landsborough." the lawman demanded. "This is United States territory."

"Is it? This is Indian country from here on. You know it, and we know it. The river divides the land. Take your law to the redskins; see what they think of it—and you—and that man there; that Gerrit. That filthy murderer who shot down a boy in his barnyard and killed an unarmed woman. This is Indian country, marshal."

It was a thing he'd thought of on the spur of the moment. The snarling river had prompted it; that, and the knowledge that the known world was behind him from now on. The lawman glared steadily for a long time, saying nothing, then he moved a little in his saddle and canted his head so that the rain hit his hatbrim instead of his hat.

"Landsborough, are you going to surrender, or do we

take you by force?" The marshal shot a significant glance at the sprawling encampment. "If you cause trouble, it'll be on your head. These people ain't above suspicion."

Before Lew could answer, Elder Mortonson spoke out in his drumroll voice. "We've been hounded and persecuted from our homes. We've been killed like swine; we've spilt our blood on land hallowed by our grandfathers in a new world where men came to worship as they pleased. Now, you come along with threats." The rain ran unnoticed off the big man's rocky face. His eyes were wells of blue fire, no longer smouldering, for there was a mighty force for wrath and combat within his breast and it had at last been reached. "Get ye down from those horses!" He thundered it, making the squalling weather a sodden background for his words. "Dismount or I'll dismount you! *Get down!*"

The marshal looked over Lew's head at the fierce patriarch of those dispossessed people who huddled up in growing numbers behind him. There was a point beyond which a man could not be driven. This was it. He knew it as he sat there feeling the water trickling down under him in the saddle. They had always run. Rarely had they ever struck back. They had despised men like Lewis Landsborough, denouncing them. There seemed no limit to their suffering, their meekness . . .

"Get down!"

It required only a glance at the wet faces and the eyes hot with fierceness. The marshal dismounted. He felt no defeat; only a dour helplessness. The creak of men getting down behind him was a sound he heard without listening to it. He watched the Mormons fanning out. Knew they were surrounding his possemen. "You're a fool, mister," he said. "You're resistin' the law. The Army'll come after you for this."

Elder Mortonson appeared not to have heard. Lew was impressed by the words, though.

He looked anxiously at the men moving around the horsemen. He saw Gerrit's blanched, frightened face. The surging reek of vengeance clawed at his vitals. He wanted to kill the man—but this wasn't right. Not when the people had come this far. Not when they were at long last beyond the hands of their persecutors with only the road to Zion ahead.

He went back to Mortonson's place and planted himself directly in front of the wild eyes.

"You can't do it. Listen to me; what you've always condemned me for is what you're doing now. One man isn't much price for all the people. You can't endanger them. Don't bring the Army down on them. Not this close to salvation."

Old Jakob's dry look clung to the younger man's face. Slowly it went to the Elder's set, ashen features. He reached out and touched his brother's sleeve. The water ran in a steady, tiny stream off his hatbrim when he inclined his head. "He's right. Let them go back. Let him go with them. Don't give way to temptation."

Thus, the silence descended and held, and only the increasing fervour of the new-come storm broke it. No one spoke except with the mute eloquence of their eyes. The sound of the heavens and the earth were all around them; wet, muddy sounds of horses moving their hooves and men shifting their weight so that the squishing, seeping sounds of weight on wet earth added to the soughing of the wind and the heavy droplets of rain that slanted like stinging whiplashes and cut them all.

Elder Mortonson was forced to meet Lew's glance. He met it, but there was a stubbornness, an ironness to it that wouldn't bend or break. Lew spoke slowly. Only a few heard him.

"You asked me to go to Zion with you. You asked me to give over my vengeance. I've agreed. Now, you're doing exactly what you don't believe I should do. Well,

I'm going back with them, and if you stop them, your God will punish all of these people. You believe that."

"They'll hang you."

"Maybe they will. Better one hung man than a hundred massacred. You've asked me to join you, and I've agreed. Now *I* ask you to say a prayer to your God. Beyond that, care for my cousin and hope for the best."

He turned away from the Mormon men and looked at the marshal. The dour man was watching them all with no particular fear in his face. Rather, he looked uncomfortable from the rain that soaked him and ran cold under his clothing from his neckline, and he had a strange tiredness showing in his eyes. Lew went over by him.

"I'll go back with you."

The marshal didn't move. He held his reins in one gloved fist and studied Lew's face. "Are you really Landsborough?"

"I am."

"Well," the lawman said softly, "I'll be damned."

"You didn't believe it?"

The marshal shook his head once. "No, I didn't. I figured it was just more madness. The country's full of it these days." He looked at Lew's face. "You know what you'll get, over there, in St. Joe?"

"I reckon. A lynch-trial."

The marshal stood ponderingly for a moment longer, then he looked over at the Mormons and spoke to Lew at the same time. "Are they pacified?"

"A good way to find out," Lew said, "is to start out. Come on, I'll lead the way."

"Where's your horse?"

"It isn't far. I'll walk."

He struck out without a backward glance. The irony of his position was in him, strongly. It wasn't as improbable as it had sounded, his contention that the law had no jurisdiction beyond the widening Missouri. On that slenderest of threads he'd taken a stand, then abandoned it. There was nothing left.

He walked steadily toward the heaving ark of an old barge that moved uneasily on the cresting river. The ferryman's face was twisted with damp anxiety. He saw that and the lapping way the river was coming over its banks. Close enough to be standing in the shallow tentacles of overflow, Lew stopped and turned. The ferryman called to him.

"Get 'em movin'. Goddamn it, it's risin' fast. Tell 'em to hurry. I dassn't wait any longer."

Lew heard the wind-dulled words amid the smashing of debris against the groaning sides of the barge. He didn't answer nor turn to look at the ferryman and the river. The water chilled the leather of his boots. He felt that, standing there looking back at the oncoming host of riders.

Farther back the Mormon men stood stock-still. Off to one side he could see the glistening face of Jakob Mortonson's daughter. A sharp pain writhed across the length of his brain at the sight of her, erect and unflinching and backgrounded by Caleb Bullard's bulk with the old grey blanket darkened by rain water.

The marshal was watching Lew's face. He reined up and sat slumped. Courage in anything, even a damned Mormon renegade, was still courage. Sacrifice was a virtue most frontiersmen understood, too. He inclined his head a little. "Here, climb up ahind me. The water's risin'. You'll get wet to the knees."

As though he hadn't heard, Lew turned and went into the deepening water to the edge of the sloping barge, leaned, grasped a cleat and pulled himself up on the splintery decking. Instantly he was aware of the plunging, sickening lurch of the old scow. A tremor ran through him; a foreboding.

He looked at the sky. It was darker now, with a running panic to its dismal movement, southward. The horses made solid sounds as the men rode up beside him, and the rising wind tore away the unconscious blasphemies of the chilled men who swung down and stood beside their horses.

He knew by instinct, with the first movement of the ferry after it was cast off and the men laid their strength to the draw-cable, that disaster was coming closer. He could see it the way the river sucked and smashed against the planking. It was a fright that grew slowly in a landsman. A thing he was unable to cope with, quite, until he turned and saw the same abrupt awareness in other faces. The very fear that made them all ugly and slack-mouthed, inspired him to calmness.

The ferryman's bleat of fright and anger was lost in the terrible sound of the river. The rain came in sheets, slantingly, cold and bitter.

A gigantic old tree, uprooted the Lord knew where, came dipping and swooping toward them. Lew saw it with helpless fascination. Head-on, the shaggy old roots dead-white, writhing around the battering-ram head of the thing. Riding the curling, casually formidable crest of the swelling top-thrust of water, the tree came swiftly, undeviatingly, rushing as though eager to smash the scow.

He wasn't conscious of yelling until he heard his own voice over the wildness of the storm. Another voice arose, even higher, more frantic and shrill. It rang with frenetic panic. Lew looked. The ferryman was clinging like a dying man, knees bent, face ghastly in the fish-belly colour of the day, eyes bulging, watching the awful course of the onrushing tree. He swung towards the man with an oath and shouted over the howl of the storm for the possemen to haul harder on the draw-cable. Even when he shouted the loudest though, he knew the futility of their labours. A crazy patchwork of terrified faces were toward him. He dimly saw the marshal's wide open mouth and wispy hair blowing damply from a head that no longer had a hat.

He swung back toward the gigantic tree. It was coming

as straight as an arrow. The river was rising so fast now they could actually feel the barge lifting. Suspended between heaven and earth, riding the heaving bosom of a nature writhing in terrifying torment, there was nothing they could do.

Lew shot a wild look at the St. Joseph side. They weren't quite half-way across; closer, actually, to the Mormon side and yet a long way from that, too. In that brief second before the great tree struck, he saw the Mormons running through their camp. Men a-horseback were racing along the far side of the river.

The wildest activity was everywhere—except beside him, where a lull, even in the wind, seemed to grip everything. He looked back at the tree. Its mighty butt with the shredded roots hanging like dying snakes, white and pulpy looking, was yards away. A lift of the maddened river jutted the thing high. It was huge; blotted out the sky for a second before it lowered itself like a furious bull, and plunged savagely at the reeling barge.

The impact was a staggering, thunderous calamity. Lew never knew whether it was thunder overhead in the leaden skies, or the meeting of the barge with its killer, that made his ears fill with sound. Horses screamed in mortal fright and men's cries rang shrilly. The awful second when the draw-cable snapped like rotten cord added its whipping howl to the tumult. The barge swung reelingly, wildly, and tilted far up with the immense tree butt embedded in its bowels.

Lew held desperately to the trembling railing. The scow lifted higher and higher and the muddy water clawed ragingly at it. He heard men and animals screaming. The sounds were lost in a wild smashing of wind against the wreckage.

He felt the planking under him quivering with a sickening heave and swung to see behind him There wasn't a horse left, and only two men still clung to the broken hull.

Both of those were hip deep in Missouri torrent. Then there was only one.

He knew the barge was going over. The last mighty surge of the river tilted it even higher. He had a strangely calm, lucid moment when he could see things with a glaring clearness, then he looked swiftly up at the raging heavens and let go.

The water came swiftly. Something smashed him an agonising blow in the back. He careened off it and the muddy force of a great, swirling weight closed over him with a congealing coldness.

He was in the wild river.

It spun and twisted him, and finally, with a depraved caprice, tossed him up above the surface. He struck out without thought, fighting to stay above the water and glad that only his boots would weight him down. The pressure was thick, like being ground between two forces of moving sand soggy with dampness. His lungs burned and his shoulders hurt from the object that had struck him when he went under.

Ahead he saw the widening breach of land and water and fought to ride the waves anglingly toward it. His head was clear and without panic, so when he could move no more, he knew he was mired.

The slime was like tar between his fingers. It held him almost motionless. He floundered with fast failing strength. Then, out of nowhere, came a force that dragged him bodily through the mud. He fought to hold his head up, and saw the taut lariat, followed it with his eyes to the straining rump of a horse with a man turned sideways high above. The face was familiar, but not the tense, horror-stricken look it wore. Danton Mills.

He got up when he was able and worked the lariat off his body and walked dumbly toward a big fire. The wagons were moving, but men were around the fire feeding it.

The exodus was a strange sight, but the river made it mandatory. His strength came back quickly, with the effervescence of youth, and by the time hands were laid on him and the heat burned through his sodden clothing to blue flesh beneath, he was feeling better. There was a fogginess to his vision and the air he sucked into his lungs cut like ice, but he stood wide-legged, dripping, feeling the return of his strength.

"Coffee. Drink it hot."

He took the cup and only belatedly looked up into the face. "Caleb. Thanks." His cousin looked quickly away from him as though he didn't want Lew to thank him. He went on by toward another man who came up reelingly.

Lew drank and turned slowly to look at the river. It was a solid wall of water with a slightly concave crest that flashed by with startling rapidity. He drank his coffee, feeling the warmth stealing into him—and he saw the bobbing head.

A man—no, two men—caught in the sunken wreckage of the huge old tree and held imprisoned in the tentacle-like roots. Fighting with weakening strength, they were hopelessly snarled. Lew finished his coffee and kicked off his boots. He turned to a man with a rider's poncho over him. "You got a knife, pardner?"

"Sure." The man stooped, groped inside his boot and came up with a wicked dagger. He didn't know what Lew wanted the thing for, and his curiosity turned to alarm when the renegade trotted back toward the water. He let out a mighty shout. Other men turned and were caught in the drama of the rescue.

Lew put the knife between his teeth and fought through the mud until the water would hold him. He was far above the partly submerged wreckage. Instinctive calculation told him where the rush of water would carry him.

He had no time to guess again, once the suction of the current had him in its swirling, wild and racing grip. It was all he could do to keep his body afloat. The undertows came ripplingly across the water like hungry snakes. They broke the surface with an oily backwash, were consumed by the current and sent back under again.

He held the knife with a clenched-jaw grip and used his strength only to guide himself and fight clear of the suction. The powerful pressure squeezed him unmercifully until he was close to the quaking hulk of the submerged wreckage, then the current was forced to either side of the log and the pressure lessened.

With groping, stiff-blue fingers he felt for a hold, found one with a slippery tenacity and worked his way along the submerged trunk until it came above water. After that he was cut by the icy wind and the cutting rain as he crawled, half-numb, along the great bole of the tree.

At the butt he could see the two men looking up at him with animal pleading in their faces. He went as low as he dared, took the knife and slashed at the snarl of roots. One of them howled up to him, but the words were whipped away. Lew could feel the quaking of the tree. He guessed the thing was entrapped with part of the barge's wreckage so that the raging force of the water couldn't tear it loose. He also surmised that, in time, the tremendous power would undermine the mud and wash the whole thing away. Because of that, he worked fast with the rain spray beating itself like miniature fists against his face.

The roots were slimy from long immersion, but the boot-knife was razor-sharp. He risked a lower foothold and bent to slash closer to the men. One of them had fought his way up high enough so that the water lapped his waist. Lew looked into the bulging eyes, and paused. Gerrit!

A surge, of hatred flared in him. It must have showed in his face, for Gerrit lowered himself, his mouth shaking with a bluish, terrorised expression. Lew looked at the other man. His head was down, mostly awash. It lolled with an ominous quietude. He yelled at Gerrit.

"Get down there! Hold his head up!"

Gerrit obeyed. He yanked the man's head back by the sparse hair and glared with bloodshot eyes, upwards. Lew's mouth trembled with the cold in spite of the clamped-down set of his jaws. He worked frantically, feeling the sinister lazy rise and fall of the big tree. Closer, ever closer, until he was beside Gerrit, hacking and slashing at the whipping roots, then the night-rider croaked fearfully in his ear.

"I'm loose. I'm loose. I got a hold here. I can get free."

Without answering, Lew avoided the man's eyes, reached far around and took the other man's shoulder in his grip and pulled him around Gerrit until he was close. Very carefully he inserted the knife under the man's woollen coat and cut downward until he felt the bottom hem. Just as carefully he slit the arms and fought the cloth away. It floated for a moment, then sunk like rock. Not until then did he look at Gerrit. His eyes were perfectly calm.

"Don't fight it. Let it carry you on an angle toward the shore. The Mormons'll snake you out, but remember, don't fight it! Go on."

Gerrit went with a wild scream that echoed strangely. Lew watched dispassionately when the water closed over him. He waited for the head to re-appear, saw it bob up and the threshing of the man's stroke, then turned back to the man he was holding against the tree. The man's eyes were defeated-looking. Lew returned the stare for a moment. He dropped the bootknife into his rear pocket, lifted his hand very methodically—and struck the man across the mouth, hard.

"You've got a chance, marshal. Kick off your boots."

The tree shifted a little. Lew's heart lurched and his

stomach tightened up as if it was a fist. "Hurry, dammit. Are they off?"

"Yes; but—I'm done. I can't—make it."

"You'll make it," Lew said harshly. "You'll make it because you've got to. Now listen : don't fight the current. Don't try to swim straight for the shore. Let the current push you all it wants to. Just paddle enough to keep your head up and steer so's you'll angle toward the Mormon side. You understand?"

"I understand, but I don't think I can—"

"Save your wind," Lew said savagely. "Are you ready? I'll be behind you. *Don't fight it!*"

"I'm ready."

With a power of ruthlessness, Lew wrenched the lawman from his hold of the gently bobbing tree, with its almost sinister laziness of water-logged motion, and gave him a heave out into the current.

He trod the icy water and allowed himself one mighty trembling quiver from head to heel, then fought against the next numbing chill and watched the lawman. The river picked him up and threw him askew into its current. Lew cursed, took a long breath and shoved out away from the tree.

He renewed his battle against the current and found himself sluggish. For a second panic threatened, but he quelled it on the rise and beat his way by force alone toward the floundering lawman.

Close enough, he reached out and grasped the lawman's shoulder. He turned him by desperation and force toward the shore. In some way he never recalled afterward, he shepherded the half-drowned man into the mud and slime, then writhed around in front, grabbed his thin hair and held his head up with the last of his own strength.

Chapter Four

It was the uncomfortable movement, harsh and jolting, that awakened Lew. He looked straight up at a mass of moving canvas, dirty beyond redemption. There were huge bows like ribs, that held the canvas up. He was in a Conestoga, and it was moving.

It was warm under the quilts, but his face was cold, especially his nose. He had a complaint in his stomach. A queasy, griping sensation. He looked at the belongings stacked around him and recognised none of them. He raised up on one elbow and felt an irresistible urge to yawn. The moving pain in his nether regions responded with a quickening anguish and he tightened up his muscles against it.

"Lew? You awake?"

He twisted his head toward the squatting man there with the dank hair hanging forlornly. "I'm awake, Cal. Where are we?"

"Going, Lew. Rolling for Zion."

He looked at his cousin. Saw the near-vacantness of the dark, liquid stare, and felt fearful before it. "To Zion," he echoed feebly. "Everyone goin', Cal?"

"All the Saints," Lew.

There was an alkali taste in his mouth. "Where's the posse from St. Joseph?"

"Oh, they stayed back by the river." The dark eyes dropped to Lew's face and assumed a close, sardonic look. "They were glad, I reckon."

"What about, Cal?"

His cousin smiled then. A wide, vastly amused smile that indicated a great, inner, secretive humour. "They got back twenty-two horses. Three of them was drowned, Lew. The rest was glad to get Mormon coffee and vittals and lie next to the fire. Elder Mortonson told 'em we weren't going to unharness when we were past the flood waters. Lew? None of 'em said anything. Not even the marshal. We kept 'em rolling, Lew. We must be fifty miles from the river by now."

Lew blinked. "Fifty miles? Cal; not that far. Man, that's close to three days travel."

Cal's smile vanished and a shred of defensiveness showed in its stead. "Well," he said, mildly, "we been rolling for over two days, Lew."

"No! You mean I been in here close to three days?"

Cal nodded sombrely. "Yep, and I've been your nurse. Lew, you've been a trial. You got the dysentery from gulping that river water. You been a trial, damned if you haven't."

Lew was struck by the rueful way his cousin said it. He smiled, seeing Cal's forlorn look, then he laughed and the pain in his stomach flared up to choke him off. He gasped. "Three days. Cal? Was I sick?"

"Sick? You were a mess. All blue and shaking like you'd fly apart. Missy and I had a time with you, Lew."

"Missy? Is that her name?"

"Melissa. They call her Missy."

"Oh." The enormity of it struck him. "She—you let her fret over me, too?"

Cal frowned the smallest bit. "The other way around, Lew. *She* let *me* help. She was here right up until a couple of hours ago. She give out then and went off to our wagon. She's tuckered." The humour showed briefly again. "Missy was your doctor; I was your nurse. You hungry, Lew?"

"It'll keep, Cal. When'll we stop?"

"Few more hours. It'll be sundown then. We'll camp."

Lew lay back after that, thinking. It might have been gratitude that made the marshal let the Mormons go on with him. He doubted that, knowing lawmen, generally. It probably was the knowledge that they were marooned across from their town and one more mouth to feed, especially a delirious one, would be more than they'd bargained for. Whatever it was, Lew had no illusions. They'd still come after him. He felt the wagon slow a little, lurch and tremble over a rock or through a buffalo wallow, and stop. He glanced up swiftly, but Caleb was gone and the tail-gate canvas flapped.

A swift rush of energy deluded him. He sat up and groped for his clothes. They weren't there; just his boots, caked with mud and stiff. He took them up and worked the leather with his hands, waiting. But it wasn't her face, when a head poked in through the canvas, it was old Jakob Mortonson, whose tired eyes looked steadily at him. Behind Jakob was Cal, moving restlessly and clutching a blanket-shawl to his shoulders.

"How do you feel?"

Lew regarded the older man dourly. "As well as a man can who has tried to drink the Missouri river dry."

"Can you walk?"

"I reckon. But I've got no clothes."

Mortonson's head disappeared. Cal stood in the opening looking doubtful. "Lew? Missy's coming."

Lew dropped down and pulled up the quilt and waited. The girl came from the front end of the wagon though, so he was still staring aft when he heard her moving behind him. Their eyes met. He noticed the blue lines under her eyes and wondered if tiredness always showed on her like that.

"Are you hungry?"

He shook his head negatively. "Not especially. Why?"

"I wanted you to say yes. My mother used to say a sick man's mending when he's hungry."

"In that case," he said gravely, "I'm hungry." He wanted to thank her some way, but the right words wouldn't come, so he looked dumbly at her. She smiled and knelt and pushed at the quilts around him without looking at his face. "They're making the fires. I'll get you some stew in a bit."

Cal cleared his throat. She swung and looked at him. "Jakob's coming with some clothes for him, Missy."

"Oh." She got up hurriedly and looked down at him speculatively. "You were very brave. We're all very proud of you."

He almost made a saturnine comment and caught it just in time. "I—it wasn't much."

She left him after that, and Jakob Mortonson came to the tail-gate with a bundle of clothing. He threw it inside and regarded Lew steadily. "They'd like to see you at the fire, if you can make it."

"I'll be there," Lew said, then, caught by something in the old man's voice, he looked up swiftly. "Why?"

Jakob shook his shaggy head. "It'll keep." He walked away.

Cal had to help Lew. The spirit was more than willing, but the flesh was woefully weak. He got dressed and was surprised to find the cramps gone. Then he tried to stand up, and his legs were like buffalo entrails filled with fluid. They wouldn't stay erect. Cal grunted under the strain of holding him, and finally let him down.

"You can't make it, Lew. I'll fetch you some stew."

"I'll make it, dammit all. Give me another boost." He made it, but Cal was perspiring from the effort by the time they were both outside the wagon. Lew's strength came slowly. He had to rest six times before he got to the circle where the Mortonsons, Danton Mills and a few others squatted, eating and waiting.

He forced himself to go unaided the last fifty feet. It seemed a mile and all uphill. He sank down with a feeling he'd never be able to rise again. Charley Crawford was beside him, a factor that made Lew feel no especial warmth. Crawford held out a bowl with a metal spoon in it. He was smiling at Lew.

"Bear meat stew with real salt in it."

Lew took it and ate. His hunger was quickly stilled, though. He wasn't as hungry as he had thought he should be. Laying aside the bowl, he looked up and was snared in Elder Mortonson's glance. The Mormon leader began his address, as he usually did, without preliminaries.

"Have you heard how you came to be here?"

"My cousin told me. They didn't try to keep me back."

"Partly," Mortonson said. "We couldn't leave you with them, mainly. You'd of died back there. I told them that."

"They'll be along," Lew said softly.

Elder Mortonson nodded his head. "Yes. We told them the route we were going. It isn't our intention to shield you, exactly. We couldn't afford to lay over, and they were in no condition to care for a dying man."

"Did that marshal object?"

"No," Mortonson said slowly, looking into the fire with a hint of ironic humour in his bold eyes. "All he said was, that you are still an outlaw in the eyes of the law." The man's face lifted. The dying day was behind him. The firelight outlined his rugged features and he resembled an ancient patriarch out of the biblical epoch, squatting with his tribesmen. "They'll be after you."

Lew felt the old curse stirring within him. Whomsoever he touched he destroyed. "When I'm able, I'll ride on. Where's my black horse?"

Mortonson didn't answer right away. He stared at Lew across the fire. "Your horse? He's with our loose-stock." There was a pause. "Why will you ride off? To save us?"

"Maybe," Lew said tartly. "Also, to save myself. I offered to give myself up. Did it, in fact. Well, I'm still a free man and I don't believe I want to go back to St. Joseph, Missouri, now. Not after I'm this far overland."

"Where will you go?"

"To Zion."

"Alone? You'll never make it."

Lew smiled crookedly. "I think a man a-horseback, travelling fast, will make better time than your wagon train."

"Better time," Mortonson said, "but that's all. There are hostile Indians all around us. You wouldn't get ten miles."

"I'll have to take the chance."

"I think not." Mortonson's gaze was level and frank. "That's why we asked you to come here. You've proven yourself in our eyes. In the eyes of our God; in the eyes of your parents' God; in the eyes of the God *you* believe in, whether you'll acknowledge such belief or not. We want you to stay among us. We are brothers one to the other."

"That's crazy," Lew said angrily. "I told you before, if I'm around it'll bring trouble to you." He looked past the Elder to old Jakob. "Ask your brother. Anyone I'm around comes to grief."

Elder Mortonson shook his head slowly back and forth. His eyes had a mystic strangeness to them. "No!" It was the same thundering way he had of speaking when deeply moved. "Listen to me, Lewis Landsborough : back in the valleys you were a scourge to all men. It was your curse that rode you and destroyed others because of you. It would have destroyed you, too, given time.

"Across the Missouri you are a freed man. The cleansing was in the muddy waters. You saw it yourself. You went

69

in unto the ark of those men and your curse rose up and smote the waters, and the lord thy God came down and entered in unto you so that you saved those who otherwise would have been destroyed because of you. Your destiny is no longer evil. You have crossed that river and left your sins behind!

"Didn't you agree to come to Zion with us? There was your affirmation before your father's God; and He heard and came to wrestle out the evil and make you great and humble, brave and dying in His guidance. You are cleansed, Brother Landsborough! You are cleansed and the devil has gone out from you. You are a brother to us. We want you to go unto Zion as our brother."

Totally at a loss, Lew avoided their glances. He could see in the embers of the low-burning fire a poetic rationality in what Mortonson said. It made him wonder—and doubt, very much.

"Speak up, brother."

He lifted his glance. It was sardonic, almost cynical. "I saved two men. Anyone could have done it who saw them out there. That proves nothing."

"Doesn't it?" Mortonson said, leaning over and with the very force of his personality, making the roll of his voice carry even when he spoke softly. "Doesn't it? Then tell me—why weren't you ever before able to save a life? Tell me why those you loved the most were destroyed in your presence? Answer me!"

Lew didn't. He got up without an awareness of that small miracle in itself. He turned his back on them and walked all the way back to the old Conestoga wagon, and sank down beside it in the chilly night. Sat there with an anguished turmoil raging worse than any fever.

"Lewis?"

He saw her materialise out of the darkness with the myriad orange-red flares of campfires behind her like a world burning to death on a far horizon. Listlessly, he answered.

"I'm here."

"Do you mind?" She dropped down when she said it.

"I reckon not."

"Here." She was holding out his shell-belt and its sagging, scratched, scarred old holster, burdened with the graceful pistol.

He took the thing and let it lie in his lap. "Thanks, ma'm."

Neither one of them spoke. Out of the abyss of the still night, clear as washed blue glass, came the scents of animals, cooking fires, and the wildness of the land itself. He began to speak without directing it to her, especially.

"He's a fool if he believes that. Crossing the Missouri didn't make any difference. Saving those men wasn't anything. Others could have done it. We all knew that storm was coming. That's the kind of stuff the Indians back home in the rain forests used to believe in. That's superstition, not religion."

She said : "Have you ever saved a life before?"

"I never tried to."

"No, but you've killed. You've been close when others died." She said it quietly, with a strong flow of softness to it. She said it with ruthlessness too, knowing how it would pain him. "You were never magnanimous before —were you?"

He turned quickly with a frown. "What are you talking about?"

"I watched you out there on that log." He swung away from her look almost fiercely. He stared into the vault of sky that curled inward like a black bowl with speckles of light in it. He said nothing. "You've been a triggerman. Maybe you still are. I don't think so. Elder Mortonson doesn't think so."

He remembered the dull, veiled hostility of Jakob's

glance. "How about the Elder's brother? How about Cal? Do you remember he wouldn't shake hands with me? It's the evil. I know it's in me. I've known it for a long time. Mortonson called it a curse; that's what it is, too."

"Jakob is waiting. He's slower; we all know him. He's gloomy. He's lived a long time and has suffered a lot. Give him time." She watched his angry profile in the watery light.

"As for Caleb, you're wrong there. Haven't you noticed it? He accepts you. You're not being fair to him, either. Think back only a few months. He was tied up in ropes then. Surely you appreciate how he's come out of it." She turned fully, sitting there beside him, and looked up into his face with her quick intensity. He could feel it— hear it in her voice—without turning to look down at her.

"You're being unfair to everyone, Lewis, but mostly, you're not being fair to yourself."

"That's enough," he said, finally. "You talked me into staying once. I stayed. This time I won't. Listen, the Saints'll have trouble to spare ahead. If I stay they'll have it behind them, too. Those men'll come back. If not them, then others like them. Authority of some kind. Don't forget I'm an outlaw to them, and they have both the power and the right to come get me." He turned slowly and looked at her. She hadn't moved. He felt the stillness of her look; the way it penetrated. He looked away swiftly.

"No matter what I do now it won't undo what I did to the men who killed my parents. Don't you see, Melissa? As long as I'm alive that curse will be with me and I'll bring it to people, like you and Cal, who shouldn't be made to suffer."

She didn't say a word back to him. They sat there for a long time in stony silence, hardly moving. The chill came down around them. He could feel a stiffness growing in his cramped legs. He got a firm hold on the wagon and lifted himself and leaned back to hide his weakness from her. She stood up then, too, and gazed up into his face.

"Good night."

He nodded without speaking. She was quickly swallowed up in the night and he let out a long-withheld breath. It made a ragged sound.

He stood until his legs had their circulation back, then he groped for the tail-gate of the big wagon, hauled himself over it and felt for the quilts. A voice came softly to him out of the darkness, so close he felt instinctively for the dangling holster.

"Lew, you're all wrong. It's like Elder Mortonson said. You've been cleansed. The road to Zion will prove it."

There was a deep, masculine timbre to Caleb's voice. He hadn't ever heard it before. A thoughtful slowness without trace of the refuge his rationale had sought after the brutal slaughter of his parents and brother. Lew was caught unawares. He sank down on his pallet, searching out the bulk of his cousin.

"You were listening to us, weren't you?"

Caleb raised up a little. His dark eyes reflected the vague night-light. "I couldn't help it, Lew. Anyway, what she told you is what Elder Mortonson said in front of all of us. It's the truth, too."

"You want me to stay, too?"

"Lew, it isn't a matter of what we all want, you know that. It's what you'll do. These are *your* people just like they're mine. They're the only people either of us have left. Your place is here, with them. Don't throw away this chance, Lew; it may be your last one."

"And what about the law that'll be after me?"

"It won't be the law. Not way out here in Indian country. It'll be the Army."

"Law, Army, it's all the same."

"I reckon," Cal said. "But if you run this time, Lew, you'll be lost. Anyway, they'll trail you to the ends of the earth. Running isn't going to help you any."

"Hell," Lew swore fervidly, "I know that, Cal. I'm not running from the law so much as trying to get away where they'll take me alone. Staying with this wagon train'll bring down the curse on them, too. They'll resist the law, or the Army, or whoever comes after me. You can see that. Elder Mortonson as much as said so—as much as did it, back by the Missouri."

Cal dropped lower in his blankets. He was silent for a moment, and somewhere, a long way off, a prairie wolf sounded. It was an eerie, lonely sound. "I tell you this, Lew. There'll be no bloodshed over you when the Army comes up with us. Mark me, Lew. There'll be no bloodshed over *you*. I don't know how I know this, but that's how it'll be. Now, go to sleep; you'll have to roll out at dawn with me and help yoke up the oxen. We want to make good time over this flat country. I hope the weather'll hold. Good night, Lew."

"Good night, Cal."

He lay back wide awake and unable to fathom the almost prophetic way his cousin had spoken. It made him uneasy and deeply stirred. He didn't sleep right up to the moment someone out in the grey dawn hit a triangle with a metal bar and sent the echoes charging like blind horsemen all through the camp. Cal awoke with a grunt and a sigh and rolled out of his quilts, sleep-stiffened fingers feeling for his boots.

"You awake, Lew?"

"I'm getting up."

The men worked without speaking for the most part, and the women made fires that burned like sullen little red eyes low on the ground, then they all ate together and the oxen stood dull-eyed, patiently, waiting for the goads and drover's whips to signal another day's toil toward the Promised Land.

Lew stood back watching them line out. Listening to the creak and groan and straining sounds of the huge and

74

awkward Conestogas; to the less noisy Red River carts; to the wagons and the sound of loose-stock being driven. He stood without moving until someone held out the split-reins to a black horse no longer gaunt, but filled out and alert-looking. He accepted the reins and turned with words of thanks. Melissa Mortonson.

"I'll ride with you, if you wish."

He knew no way to refuse, so he swung up into the saddle and watched her mount astride. It still startled him to see a woman—a girl—ride like that. She waited in silence and patience until he reined out beside the wagons, then she urged her sorrel horse, too.

They rode through the grey, misty dawn with its innumerable sounds hardly ruffling its immense stillness. Neither spoke until the sun fought triumphantly with the night and came higher, so that its prismatic brilliance shone off each drop of the dew they rode through, so that the wetness was a fairy necklace of transparent pearls. Then she spoke, and the sound was like a little girl's voice, to him. Humbly thankful.

"I'm glad you stayed."

He answered with gruffness he didn't feel. "Did you expect me to ride away in the night?"

"Yes, I did."

Startled, he swung and looked at her. The fresh-scrubbed shine of her face was wholesome-looking. There was a shy look in her eyes.

"Well, why would I do that? I can ride off any time. Right now, for a fact."

"I know you can."

"I'm beholden to no man," he said.

"I know that, too."

"Then you needn't worry about me slipping away in the night."

"I'm glad you won't."

"I didn't say I *wouldn't*—just that I don't *have* to."

"Yes," she said swiftly. Just that one word and no more.

He rode with the warming sun on his back and a faint rustling of disquietude in his heart. He didn't look around at her again until Danton Mills rode up and eyed them both with a patently false glance of casualness. Lew saw it because he had long ago developed the instinct to observe things. It ruffled him a little, but he said nothing.

They rode with only desultory conversation, and the monotony of the vast spaces became a part of them. Day jogged after day in this unvarying flatness. They were shaken out of their thralldom only when confronted with the brooding ruggedness of their first mountain pass, aloof and mighty, dark and forbidding, directly before the first wagon.

Elder Mortonson rode slowly back down the line to where Lew sat his black horse, watching the great serpentine come to a jolting halt. He didn't see the leader until Mortonson swung in toward him, then he was arrested by the typical bluntness of the man; his way of speaking without preliminaries, without even the courtesy of formal address.

"There's work ahead. We've been considering something in council and I might as well tell you now. Beyond these mountains is hostile country. We've need of strong men from here on. I want you to pick some of the younger men who have good horses and ride yonder." He motioned with his arm beyond the bleak mountains that challenged them. "Scout out the land."

Lew nodded impassively. "How'll the wagons get over?"

"We've had men out scouting a pass since early in the day. They've not returned, but we've the Lord's guidance. They'll find a way."

And they did, to Lew's surprise. He and Danton Mills and eleven other armed Mormons met them on their return. They smiled and pointed the way southward, where a cataclysm of nature in eons gone had shattered and rent a passageway as though for outpouring waters.

Lew made for it, troubled in mind. In a puzzled way he hated himself for staying, and in another way he was strongly held by the temptation to remain all the way to Zion. It was the indecision that plagued him night and day so that Melissa saw it, as did Cal. Others too, but without understanding it.

They found the trail and marvelled. With only a little trouble the largest of Conestogas would be able to pass over the boulder-strewn trail. Lew hauled up short, half-way through the pass. Danton Mills reined over.

"What is it?"

"That," Lew said, pointing down at a freshly-made track of an unshod horse.

Mills leaned out and stared with a gathering frown. Lew looked upward, along the craggy overhead where the frowning rocks could conceal a savage. His skin crawled under his hat and he longed to ride clear of the place. If an ambush was in the making, there was no better spot. He reached over and nudged Danton Mills.

"Come on, follow me."

He set his horse into an easy lope and rode zig-zag among the boulders until the steep incline of the pass made him slow a little, but by then he was beyond the point where danger might have lurked. Stopping on the edge of the prairie above, Lew swung his horse and waited for the others. They clattered up and Danton Mills was ranging the rocks with a worried expression.

Lew could see the entire dramatic, staggering distances below and outward, down over the land they had traversed. By turning, he could see another plateau, stepped up higher, that lay even farther inland from the passageway. Without knowing it, he was on an ancient trail used by raiding neolithics since the dawn of time. He breathed deeply of the scented air and looked for the pines he could smell.

They were south of the pass a few miles, banks and tiers of them stair-stepping their way up a mountain slope that fell away from the prairie like a gaunt black snake.

"Now what?" Danton Mills' eyes were still troubled beneath the cliff of his brow, where shaggy eyebrows grew. "If there's Indians around, we'd best not split up, had we, Lew?"

"I reckon not, but there's no sense in all of us going up that hill, either. You take three or four men and sashay up there. See if you can find any more tracks. I've got a feeling—"

"Me, too," Mills interrupted hastily. "Slocum, you and Crawford and Churchill come with me."

Lew dismounted and squatted beside his horse. The other men followed his example. They could see Mills and the other Mormons almost all the way to the top. It was a long wait and a silent one. The brooding land with its agelessness seemed to resent their presence. Mills came back slowly, more puzzled-looking than ever. He met Lew's glance with a grunt, swung down and stood beside his horse, hip-shot, looking off into nothingness.

"They were up there all right. Not a lot of 'em, but enough to make a man ponder."

"Indians?"

Mills looked into Lew's unruffled glance. "Yes, Indians."

Lew got up slowly and glanced over the land. There was no point in riding their horses down, hunting for anything as elusive as an Indian who didn't want to be seen. He had the self-conscious sensation of being watched. It irked him. "Danton, you ride back and show the way for the wagons. Tell them to send men with bars and ropes to snake the boulders clear of the trail. We'll stay up here, just in case."

Mills mounted and rode slowly back the way they had all come. Lew squatted again. The men with him slouched with an outward appearance of lassitude that fooled no one. Lew decided if the redskins were loitering, they'd be back there in those trees. The distances were deceptive in the clear, sparkling air. He shifted uneasily and wished he had a rifle as well as a pistol.

It was a good two hours later when he heard the first yoke of oxen straining with their cumbersome cargo, up through the pass. His men watched as the train lunged and settled, fought free and groaned its way, toilingly, upwards. Three times wagons had to be double-yoked in order to make it up the last few hundred yards, but by then the majority of the great caravan was in the knee-high old grass and the sun was sinking, a bloody disc off in the west.

Elder Mortonson sought Lew with his habitual bluntness. His eyes were steely and untired, for all the day's exertion. "Could it be those tracks you men saw were white men?"

"I reckon," Lew said, laconically. "only I can't figure a white man riding a barefoot horse in rocky country like this."

Mortonson was silenced by that. He walked away with his shoulders squared, as though to meet the perils of the night head-on. Lew heard him order the men to make a wagon-corral of all the wagons with the loose-stock inside. It was done that way and the night closed down upon them.

The hours passed.

There was a deathly quiet as the last light failed. The people moved like spirits, soft-walking and with a depth of fear in them. Over by the wagon of Jakob Mortonson, the Elder sat with a desolateness in him. They all had it, Lew saw. Fear. Not of the known, for none of them feared that any more, not these people who had been driven out of their homes and seen their loved ones shot down in the night; it was fear of the *un*known that held them now. He felt it a little himself, and was glad when Caleb came over with a long musket in his big hand, and smiled boyishly as he dropped down.

79

"Been lookin' at the maps. They aren't as good as some I've seen."

"I reckon not; especially if they bought 'em in St. Joseph. Those gentiles'd sell a man anything for money; anything at all."

Caleb shrugged as though unwilling to go quite that far. "Well, they show us a long way from St. Joseph—or Zion either, for all that."

"I wonder what's keeping the law."

Caleb shot him a swift, dark glance. There was bitterness and guilt and hope in it. "Maybe they won't chance it. This is far out. Those signs o' Injuns you saw to-day—any outfit less strong than we are'd be crazy to try it."

Lew looked at his dark cousin and smiled. "Funny thing about the law, Cal. It never gives up. Never. They can let a man go until he's old and grey—they'll never let him go. Come around some evenin' at supper time, or rout him out of a deep slumber in the night—the law never gives up, Cal."

"Not back there," Caleb said with a toss of his head. "But this is different. You've got thousands of miles of redskin-country 'tween you an' them, Lew. They'd have to want you awful bad to chance it."

"They'd chance it all right. I'm a murderer to them, don't forget that."

"But there's no reward, Lew," Caleb said, pained. "They manhunt mostly for rewards, those gentiles. I don't expect they'll even try, now."

Lew looked over the glow of the cooking fires where men with guns were making rounds. He knew that others were beyond the wagons, out there in the mysterious, frightening night. He knew, too, that the chill late autumn days that lay ahead would hold no peace at any time. Only eternal vigilance—and the size of their wagon-train—would bring them safe to Zion. They would be plodding endlessly, dipping and rising and following the contours of endlessness itself, moving forever out into the cold grey horizon, farther and farther . . .

"Lewis."

He knew her before he looked up. "Yes'm?"

"Tell me about the Indian."

"Indian? Ma'm, I didn't see any Indian; just a horse track. Could've been a white man."

"Could've been an Indian scouting party, too, couldn't it?"

He didn't answer. Caleb lay in the reflected heat of the fires and watched them both, his dark, soft eyes taking on glowing awareness. He answered for his cousin.

"Could've been, Missy. Could've been an' more'n likely was. But we're strong." Caleb rolled his shaggy head to include the fire-lighted, huge circle with its horde of people and the bristle of their armament. "Those are our family, Missy. Our sinews and our strength. So long's we got those, I don't reckon a war band'll bother us much."

Lew listened to Cal and turned his head very slowly to look at him. The strong head on its thick neck was resting easily, lolled a little, as though in comfortable repose and pleasant relaxation. There was no agitation in the sombre glance of the dark-liquid eyes. He sought for signs of tension and found none. He looked away, and the girl stood up beside him.

"If it's only Indians, I'm glad." She said it with a possessive fierceness that made him look up at her swiftly, craning his neck to do it.

"Well, I am! We had Indians back home."

"Not," Lew said dryly, "like these, though. I've heard men talk about the Indians out here. They aren't the same at all."

"An Indian's an Indian," she said stubbornly.

"Have it like you will," he retorted, irritated.

She hesitated, then very glaringly ignored him in favour of Caleb. "There are sentinels out, Cal."

"I know. I'm to go out later."

Lew looked at his cousin swiftly, then shoved upwards to his feet and looked across the compound at the Mortonson fire. Without speaking he struck out through the clutches of people and made his way to the spot where the Mortonson brothers were eating, and dropped down.

"Don't send my cousin out there, beyond the wagons, to-night. I'll stand his watch."

Elder Mortonson gravely heaped a dented bowl and passed it in profound silence to Lew. Jakob was watching the lean, stormy face with his dull, tired glance that had the steel-flakes in the background of it.

"I said I'll stand Caleb's watch."

"We heard you," the Elder said. "Melissa's his nurse. She says its best for him to stand his watch."

"Best!" Lew exploded. "Why, he's—"

"He's capable of it." She was there by his side again. He felt an urge to rise up and shake her by the shoulders; instead, he set the bowl down gently and firmly and leaned forward with the fierceness showing in his glance. "I said I'll stand his guard. I meant it. You're hurrying him too much. He needs time. He's strong, but don't go altogether on looks. When a man's hurt inside, it doesn't heal over so quickly." He got up then and faced Melissa. "I know, ma'm."

None of them spoke. He turned and stalked angrily, bristlingly, back to his spot where Cal was drowsing, sank down with his insides churning, and didn't even see Melissa Mortonson following dutifully with two heaping bowls. And she, in her turn, didn't see the unblinking, wooden stares that followed her from the faces of Elder and Jakob Mortonson, the one her father, the other her uncle.

Chapter Five

Lew stood Cal's watch. He did it by the simple expedient of talking Cal into sleeping until his time came, then failing to waken him. He paid for it with Melissa's coldness that lasted two full days, and a later drowsiness as he rode with the wagons.

But, at the end of three days, the repercussions were past and the pretty girl was riding with him again, only she had brought another girl with her, and oddly—to Lew at any rate—this other girl, named Mary Murphy, paired off with his cousin, so that of the foursome he and Melissa Mortonson were one half, while Caleb Bullard and Mary Murphy were the other half.

He had to ride out frequently when some of the fifteen men he'd recruited and detailed for outriding came in to report signs of Indians. The exasperating part of it, though, was that they never saw a single redskin. Not even when the prairie was the flattest and the air as clear as new glass. Signs and tracks, dead little cooking fires and occasionally a spoiling carcass of a deer, an antelope, or, less frequently until they were about fourteen days' travel from the pass, buffalo carcasses. Signs of hostiles, but no hostiles.

He rode one dazzling morning far ahead with Danton Mills. They had perfected a system of signalling on sunny days with bits of glass or metal. Lew had also worked out a workable plan whereby none of the advance guard of horsemen were ever out of assistance range from the others. He had a deep feeling of unrest, of nearing peril, but he kept it to himself. There was nothing, actually, to back it up with. Mills felt the same uneasiness, though. He indicated it the time he and Lew came together on a low, rolling hummock and sat there looking back at the crawling line of wagons.

"Why don't they show themselves, Lew?"

"I don't know."

"Well, you must've thought on it, some."

Lew looked at the larger man. There was strain and sleeplessness in Mills' eyes. "I think it's one of two things, Dan. Either they're trailing us until we're far enough away from any help they think might be coming behind us, or else they're waiting until they can round up a big enough herd of warriors to jump us."

Mills nodded slowly. "That's about how I got it figured. Only I thought they might be waiting for some special place to do it in. Like a deep arroyo or another ambush spot like that pass."

"You might be right," Lew said. "You seen anything up ahead that'd work out for 'em like that?"

Mills turned a little in his saddle. "You see where the plains break off up there? Over where those mountains come south a little, then turn back?"

Lew looked. "Yeh. Is there a canyon up there?"

"Not a canyon exactly. There's a big bowl that we'll go through. It's sort of like a wide park. The hills on both sides aren't steep, but if the wagons are down in there, they can't see out on either side." Mills looked back at Lew. "It's the only place I can see where they might try it. That, or farther on. In some place we haven't scouted out yet."

Lew considered it for a moment, watching Mills' face.

"Well, how'd it be if we were to line men on both sides of the hills?"

"It'd take a lot of men, Lew."

"We'll ride over it for sign then, before the wagons get close to it. That ought to tell us what we want to know."

They left it at that. Later, when Lew was riding up the great, staggering, rocking line of wagons with Melissa, the girl said something he didn't hear, and pointed. He looked ahead, squinting. Three of his men were riding toward the Mormon train in an easy lope. Without speaking, he lifted the black horse into a long gallop and swirled past the ponderous wagons to meet them. By the time he got up in front, however, the scouts were already talking to Elder Mortonson.

"Looked to be about fifty or sixty of them," Charley Crawford was saying. He turned a little to include Lew in his report. "Indians, Lew. War party of 'em. Maybe half a hunnert."

"Where?"

"Back up the line about three miles. They're just sitting their horses up there, watching us."

Lew looked at the Elder. Mortonson was looking straight back at him. He turned his horse and jerked his head at the scouts. "Let's go back." They rode fast and Lew paid no attention to any of them until they were all back up where Danton Mills and several other scouts were talking. Then he caught Danton's startled look off to one side of him, and turned.

"Melissa!"

"Yes?" She said it demurely, with large-eyed innocence.

He glared. "You go back."

"Why?"

"Why! Why, because this is no place for a lady, that's why."

She seemed about to refuse, the way her eyes flashed

blue fire; then, just as suddenly, she dropped her glance a little.

"All right." She turned her horse and rode slowly back toward the distant wagons. Lew watched her go and felt mean. He turned back to the men in time to catch Danton Mills and Caleb exchanging a long, wry glance.

He frowned. "Show me your Indians."

They rode at a jog for another three-quarters of a mile, and he saw them. The men stopped; irked, Lew kept on riding toward the line of plumed, vivid horsemen far ahead. The others held to his slow gait. He didn't stop until he was just beyond what he estimated to be rifle-range. Sitting there in the immensity of the vast plains, the Mormons could see their adversaries very clearly. The Indians were well mounted. Only three or four had rifles. The rest had stubby little bows and quivers that bristled with tufted arrows. They were painted and decorated and extremely colourful. Lew counted them.

"Forty-five," he said to Danton Mills.

"If there's forty-five in plain sight," Mills said stonily, "there'll be a hundred more over the hill."

Lew looked beyond them to where the ground sloped away. "Is that the hollow you were telling me about? Down behind them, there?"

"Yes."

Lew studied the terrain, then swung back for another long look at the warriors. "Well, I think you were a little wrong, Dan. They aren't going to wait until the wagons go down in there. They're using that bowl to hide the rest of their army in. Either that, or they're planning on using the hollow for a sort of gathering place, hospital, and whatnot, while they make war up on the prairie."

Mills didn't answer. Charley Crawford spoke in his rasping Missouri voice. "They's a big feller out front. He must be the leader. He's hung like a Christmas tree. Look at the spangles on 'im. What kind o' Injuns ye reckon 'em to be?"

Lew looked around at Crawford. "The fighting kind," he said.

The Indians apparently had satisfied their own curiosity, for now their leader turned his head a little, said something, then started to ride toward the Mormons. Lew felt his insides tighten up.

"You boys with rifles hold 'em ready. Crawford, ride back to the wagons and tell 'em to send up about forty more men. Tell 'em to ride fast and bring all the guns they can carry."

Crawford whirled his horse and lashed it with a braided quirt. Another man eased up close to Lew in the spot Crawford had vacated. Lew turned, saw the level gaze of the man, and winced. "Cal! What're you doing here?"

"Any reason why I shouldn't be?" his cousin asked quietly, his dark eyes calm and steady-looking.

"No reason under the sun," Danton Mills said, with a long, reproving look at Lew.

"Pretty hard-lookin' bunch," a Mormon said. Lew swung back to look. The Indians, Utes, although none of the Mormons knew it at this time, were still approaching. They rode slowly, with great dignity and their trappings were flamboyant in the extreme. They were all armed to the teeth. All had steel knives. Some carried long lances tipped with murderous-looking spear-heads. Their upper bodies were painted, while their legs were encased in what appeared to be separate leggings over each leg and held at the waist by a thong that encircled the middle. Their moccasins were of soft uppers with elk or buffalo soles. Their hair was in braids, although the man who appeared to be their leader had a small topknot arrangement with a piece of white weasel skin bound around it while the balance of his hair was braided, then encased in what looked like beaver skin.

Most of the warriors carried medicine shields. These were made from the tough, incredibly thick neck-hide of bull buffaloes. They would turn an arrow easily, and a rifle ball as well, unless the range was very close.

The leader stopped his horse. The beast was painted with religious symbols and otherwise decorated to enhance his fearsomeness to an enemy. The Mormons weren't especially frightened by the panoply, but they were most certainly fascinated, for none of them had ever seen wild Indians before.

Lew studied the leader's face for the key to their purpose. Outnumbered, he nevertheless felt no immediate peril. All the same, he hoped Charley Crawford wouldn't be delayed.

The big Ute chieftain gazed impassively at the Mormons. His dark eyes missed nothing. He studied the horses, the bridles, saddles, the guns and boots, the spurs and clothing of the motionless whites; then, satisfied, he fixed Lew— who was slightly advanced from the others—with his dark glance. When he spoke it was in a halting, guttural, thoroughly incomprehensible language. Some of his words were formed with his lips, others came with a deep-rolling blast from far down his throat.

Lew smiled in spite of the gravity of the situation. He raised his hand, palm upward, and shrugged. The Indian understood and stopped speaking. Very carefully he slipped his war shield over his back, freed both hands and entered into a graceful series of finger, hand and arm manipulations that were even more puzzling to the white men. Lew shook his head again. Danton Mills swore softly, his forehead creased with perplexity.

The warrior sat back and looked at Lew for a long time; then, with a fluid movement he dismounted from his horse and motioned for Lew to do the same. Lew got down.

The Ute hunkered on his haunches and took one finger

as an indicator, and began to draw a long line between them. Completing this, he looked up at Lew. The meaning was clear enough. The Indian was on one side of the line; Lew was on the other side. Lew nodded, motioning to himself as being across the line from the Indian. The Ute studied his face—especially his eyes, which were blue and detailed, very unlike Indian eyes. Then he slowly withdrew his knife and re-traced the dividing line with it, lifted it and plunged it hard, into the middle of the line. Lew sat back on his haunches and looked at the Indian.

Danton Mills, impatient, swung down and glowered at the half-buried knife. "What's he trying to say, Lew?"

"It's simple enough, Dan. He drew that line to show that it divides us. The Indians are there, and we are here. The knife, as I understand him, means we are not to cross into Indian territory—if we do, they'll fight us."

The Indian listened to them talking. His beady glance swept from one face to the other, then he withdrew his knife, sheathed it, and stood up. He was a good four inches shorter than Danton Mills, whom he regarded with profound interest. Mills didn't return the regard, except with an angry glance.

"We've got to cross, Lew."

"I know," Lew said quietly, looking at the other warriors. "And we will, too, but let's try to work it out peaceably, first."

He looked back down the prairie. Crawford was coming. One of the Utes said something in a swift and harsh tone. Their leader stepped away from Lew and Mills, looking around them.

Lew swung his head toward the Indian. He saw the quick antagonism come into the earth-coloured face and made an exaggerated smile to reassure the warrior. The Indian turned swiftly and vaulted onto his horse's back. Sitting up there, he donned his dignity again. His face was arrogant and impassive.

Lew mounted and leaned over toward Danton Mills. "Ride back and tell them not to make a move toward their guns. If the Elder's there, send him up here. And Dan —see if they'll send someone back for some coffee—anything we can use to soften these Indians up with."

Danton shot the Indians a hard look. "We could lick 'em, Lew."

Lew straightened up in the saddle. "How do you know, Dan? How many more are down in that hollow?"

Mills turned his horse and rode stiffly away. Lew was watching the Indians. They were ignoring his little party of scouts and concentrating on the larger body of riders slowing now as they came in behind their own men. Abruptly, the war leader turned and spoke to a youth beside him with feathers notched and worked into the crown of his hair. The warrior reined away and loped easily back toward the hollow.

Lew watched him with a feeling of sardonic triumph. He heard riders come up beside him, but he ignored them, waiting. Elder Mortonson's drumroll voice spoke into the stiff silence and Lew waved away the question without looking away from the far lip of land.

It was a long wait, but his reward came when Indians began to stream up out of the sunken place. He smiled crookedly, watching them. They didn't come any closer, though. The line of them was long and, judging from the way every warrior among them was painted, armed and mounted, they had been waiting just over the hump of land; in the event there was a fight, they would have been handy.

Lew turned slowly toward the Mormon leader. "There; count them. That's their army." He watched Elder Mortonson's face and saw the grimness come into it long before Mortonson looked over at him.

"What are they up to?"

"This seems to be as far as they'll let us go." Lew nodded his head toward the warrior sitting his horse across from them, gazing fearlessly at the white men. "He's some kind of a leader. He gave me to understand with signs that we can't go any farther into Indian country."

Elder Mortonson's strong face settled into a bleakness. He eyed the Indian with a challenging look, then he leaned forward in that attitude Lew had come to know so well. Lew interrupted the Mormon leader before he could speak.

"He can't understand you."

"The heathen'll understand a gun, though."

Lew shook his head adamantly. "No; let's try something else first. We can always fall back on guns."

"What?" Mortonson's glance was fiery, his jaw jutted. He would treat with no infidel; it showed clearly in his face. The gentiles were bad enough, but these savages— they weren't even worshippers of the One God.

"I sent Danton back for some gee-gaws. Let's see if we can't buy a passage across their land."

Mortonson looked for a long time into Lew's face. Very slowly, very bitterly and bleakly, he straightened up in his saddle. He wrestled valiantly with himself, and Lew watched the battle, fascinated.

Danton Mills came back when the sun was sloping off toward the towering ramparts in the west. He had two old muskets and a bundle of food under one arm. Two older men trailed in his wake with other things. Danton looked inquiringly at Lew, and past him to the flinty profile of Elder Mortonson.

Lew nodded at him. "Get down and unroll the goods, Dan. Will those old guns shoot?"

"I reckon. We loaded them back there. At least they're better'n what those Indians are carrying."

"I wouldn't want to be behind either of them," Lew said dryly, "when they went off."

Danton got down and made up an imposing array of the goods he and the older men had carried back from the wagons. Lew watched with a perfectly blank face, and a deep inner sense of ironic amusement. Danton had chosen well, for there was a vivid splash of colour spread out in the tall grass and the Indians were eyeing it with interest. He looked up at the war leader and saw greed clearly etched in the mahogany face.

Dismounting, Lew motioned the warriors up close. They didn't wait for their commander to order it, but swung down and stalked close to the array of white man food and presents.

With a grand flourish, Lew took the best of the two old muskets, threw it to his shoulder—with a prayer and a tightening of muscles—and yanked the trigger. The gun bucked hard and belched a mighty explosion. With a smarting shoulder, Lew turned then and handed the gun to the war leader with a big smile. The Ute grasped the weapon with eyes that shone, held it at arm's length and regarded it much as he might have regarded a fork of lightning; pleased greatly, and greatly respectful.

"Show him how to charge the thing, Dan," Lew said; then, reassuming his role as father-bountiful, he ordered some of his scouts to go among the Indians with lesser presents, food, and good cheer.

Lew sweated under the failing daylight, laughed often and spent half an hour showing the Ute war leader how to aim his musket. Each time the delighted savage fired the piece, Lew winced, but evidently the old gun was better made than it appeared to be, for it didn't burst.

Watching the Indians, gauging the moment when their delight was at its peak, Lew touched the war leader's arm and drew his attention away from the musket for a moment. He squatted, took out his own knife, drew a long, wavering line between them, sheathed his knife, stood erect with a smile—and stepped over the line to indicate entering and crossing the Indians' country.

The Ute leader thought a moment, then smiled broadly, disclosing dark-coloured gums and flashing, big strong teeth. He raised a hand and put it palm inward, fingers extended against his own breast, then extended his arm and placed it over Lew's heart in the same fashion. Lew understood the intention and smilingly grasped the Ute's hand and pumped it up and down ceremoniously. This excited new interest in the Indian, who was clutching his new musket with his free hand. He made Lew repeat the gesture four times, and the fifth time took the initiative and did the pumping himself.

Lew turned toward Mortonson, saw the latent outrage in the Mormon leader's eyes, and prudently continued to enact the part of the leader of the white men. The Indians neither noticed the Elder as any one special, nor cared. They made elaborate signs for the white men to come with them to their encampment and, by simply stuffing as many of the fingers as they could get into their mouths, conveyed the idea.

Lew pointed to the sun, moved his hands over his clothing to indicate the need for better attire, smiled and turned toward his horse. The warrior, though, rushed after him, halted him with a touch, pointed to the sun himself, let his arm drop a little to indicate how much later they would meet again, then proceeded to pump Lew's hand so enthusiastically that Lew's hat worked loose on his head.

After that the two parties broke up. Riding back toward where the Mormon vehicles had already corraled, they could hear the occasional explosion of the old muskets far behind them.

Lew rode beside the Elder. He said nothing. Mortonson finally broke the silence. He sounded mortified and chagrined. "Bribing heathen. We shouldn't have dealt with them."

93

Lew had his answer ready. "Better to bribe them, Elder, than to fight them when they're strong and we have women and children with us."

"That's compromising with the godless, Lewis."

Lew smiled with his eyes only. "I reckon not. You can preach to them, Elder. You sure can't jump out into the middle of over a hundred fighting Indians with a gun in one fist and the Book in the other, and expect to make any converts."

"It's been done," Mortonson said stubbornly.

"Maybe," Lew said. "But not here. Not now, with peace and passage paid for. Carrying The Word to the Indians won't be done with guns, I don't think. Maybe they could be converted by example—I don't know—but I *do* know anyone who tries it with guns is going to get set-back a mite." Lew watched the great, ugly hulks of the Conestogas loom ahead in the gloaming.

"I don't know any more about those savages than you do, Elder, but I've seen enough to-day to know it'd be better to get along with them, than without them. Out here, any-way. After we get to Zion, we can start enlightening them. Right now I think our first job's to get there."

"That's not a very devout outlook you have," Elder Mortonson said sternly.

"I reckon you're right," Lew answered him. "Maybe I'm too realistic. I've always been that way, Elder. I probably always will be. I believe in takin' a small bite before you take a large one. One thing at a time. Zion first, Indians second."

They were close enough to see the black swarm of people watching them. Lew said no more until he had swung down within the wagon circle, then people crowded around him, but one set of eyes shone the brightest.

He parried questions by sending the most insistent folks to Elder Mortonson. He derived grim pleasure from doing

94

it, too. Melissa alone remained with him when he loosened the cincha of his black horse and let out a long sigh.

"Lew?"

"Yes?"

"Are you tired?" She was looking up at him with that disconcerting intensity; that look that always made him uneasy because it reminded him of Aunt Jem's look.

He shook his head. "No; why? Do I look tired?"

"No," she said. "I wanted to ask you something—but when you're tired you're disagreeable."

He looked away from her with a sense of guilt. He had a very clear picture of the way she had looked, small and dejected, when he'd made her ride back to the wagons. "Well, I reckon I won't be disagreeable, ma'm."

She had a high flush under her eyes. "You talked them all out of fighting, didn't you?"

He was embarrassed and annoyed. She could do that to him. "I don't expect they'd of fought, anyway." He smiled at her. "Dassn't; there was too many Indians."

"But—you did it, didn't you?"

The annoyance grew as she persisted. He turned and faced her fully with a pained, very obviously worked-over look of patience in his face. "Melissa, there wasn't going to be any fight. They didn't think we ought to cross their land. We gave them a couple of old muskets and some food and other things. They agreed we could cross their land and invited us to a sort of supper of some kind with them. That's all there—"

"Me, too? All of us?"

He was stumped. "Well, I reckon there's way too many for all of us to go. Besides, seems to me a lot of us ought to stay here and sort of watch things. I don't know about Indians. You hear a lot, you know."

"We'll go together," she said.

He looked pained again. "No; they'll get the wrong idea from that, Melissa."

95

"Well, that's all right. We'll never see them again, anyway."

He was shocked. "Them? I'm not thinking about them. I'm thinking about the people right here. Our people."

"Oh!" She looked at him wistfully. "Well, I know it was you that made peace with them, anyway."

Thoroughly aggravated, he frowned at her. "*How* do you know so much—tell me that!"

"Cal told me," she said sweetly, shot him a sidling smile and walked slowly over toward the throng of people who were clustered around her uncle. Lew watched her go with a troubled look in his face. There was a steady, deep stillness in the background of his gaze, too. A sort of anxiousness that shone in the gathering dusk.

"Lew? Say, what do we do now?"

He turned to face Cal and Danton and Charley Crawford. "Do? Why, wash up, I reckon. Put on clean shirts if you've got them, and ride over. Hell; *I* don't know. I've never sat down with a bunch of Indians before."

Cal looked doubtful. "We were just talking to old Ezra Morgan. He says Injuns make big feasts like this—out of dogs."

The sound of it made Lew's stomach churn. He considered it carefully, then looked into his cousin's worried face. "If it's dog, then I reckon we'll eat dog. I don't expect it'll *be* dog, though. Not with all the deer and buffalo they've got around here."

But it *was* dog, and very delicious dog, too, cooked with skunk-cabbage and wild mustard and a bitter paste of juniper berries that seasoned it. The freshly-scrubbed Mormons sat down and ate, using their fingers as the Utes did, dipping into the communal pot, fishing for chunks of soft meat and gorging themselves until they were all full. Then their hosts accepted their pantomimed compliments with an equally long pantomime on how the pot-pourri was made. To the lasting horror of Lew and the other white men, they were shown how puppies were fed— gorged, rather—then given a powerful cathartic to cleanse them, then killed while the last meal—heavily spiced— was still in them, and cooked.

Lew wasn't squeamish. He had been hunted and hounded back home in the rain forests too long to question the source of sustenance, but he felt queasy all the same. Not as queasy as the blanched faces around him indicated his friends to be, but close to it.

In order to avert what he feared might be an unpardonable breach of etiquette, he launched into a long harangue on friendship between the Mormons and the Indians. This was in English, but he gesticulated eloquently enough for the Utes to get a smattering of what he meant. And he accomplished his purpose, too, because the Mormons, including a white and ashen-looking Elder Mortonson, had their attention diverted when the war leader of the Utes got ponderously to his feet and launched into an altogether unintelligible and heavily punctuated dissertation of his own. The purpose appeared to be something loosely to the effect that these particular, gift-bearing white men, were assured their right to cross the Indians' country whenever they wished.

On that note, with a strong moon high and the bitter cold crisping the grass they sat upon, the conclave broke up.

Lew rode back between his cousin and Danton Mills. The big man looked at him reproachfully. "Cal told you what it'd be," he said in a mournful voice.

"I didn't really believe it, though," Lew answered. "Anyway, that's a cheap price to pay to avoid a war, isn't it?"

Neither of them answered him right away, then Caleb spoke with his head averted. "I'm not right sure, Lew. Dog!"

Lew throttled his laughter. "Did you notice the Elder's face? I figured he was going to let it up."

Danton Mills' face was wooden and unsympathetic toward the sound of amusement in Lew's voice. "He did. I saw him leaning over by his horse just before we left there."

Lew's laughter was soft and rippling. Both his cousin and Danton Mills looked at him reprovingly, almost with hostility. He choked off the laughter and they rode through the lowering night without speaking again until they were within the wagon circle, where a large body of men and women and children entered into a babble of curiosity as the feasters returned.

Lew avoided them as he always did. He led the black horse out onto the prairie beyond the circle, hobbled him and left him. There were guards farther out whose primary duty was to watch for Indians and whose secondary chore was to keep the hobbled horses between themselves and the wagon circle. That way the Mormon animals kept up their strength.

He went back into the circle and saw the last of the returning men dismounting. There were repressed peals of feminine laughter and growled sounds of irritated men. He guessed the reason, and smiled into the darkness. It had been a cheap price to pay, he thought.

Moving like a shadow against the gaunt old wagons, he went to his bedding and sank down on it, tossed his bridle over the tilted-up saddle and lay back with his hat over his face. A man could fare worse. At least he was free—they were all free. The unknown had been met and conquered.

Overhead, up through the arm-thick spokes of a giant Conestoga wheel, he could see the sky. He pushed his hat away and looked out at it. There was a brittle coldness in the night, and a stillness. It was so clear the stars seemed only an arm's length away, and every small sound boomed out like a gun shot.

A man could grow, beyond the land of the gentiles. He could stand up on his own wide legs and see God up there on nights like this. He could find a little valley or a plateau out in Zion. He could build a log house on it like the ones his folks had had back in Kelso County; or like the squat, mighty house Uncle Zack had had over in Brazo Valley. A house with honed inner logs and moss chinking; a place with a mud-wattle and sandstone hearth where the firelight made a dull warmth against the walls. Zion. There'd be a place there for a man with a strong back and willing hands.

He rolled up on his side. There was a spreading peacefulness in him. Something akin to his old loneliness, but different, in a way. A depth of peace he had never felt before. He closed his eyes tightly and felt it, like warm blood, coursing through him. Then he opened his eyes . . .

"You!"

"Do you mind?"

He blinked up at her, saying nothing. She smiled. The milky moonlight shone off her shiny face with its blue eyes and full mouth and clear complexion. "Don't you feel well, Lew?"

"I feel fine. Why shouldn't I?"

"You were rolling around on your quilts."

He blinked at her again. She wouldn't understand. He sat up and ducked away from a stretcher that ran from the front-axle of the Conestoga's running gear to the wagon-bed.

"Did you like your dog supper?"

He looked around and saw the amusement flickering in her glance. He thought of what Elder Mortonson had done and smiled. "It was good, until I knew what it was. Well, a man eats worse now and then. I don't reckon many liked it afterwards, though. Your uncle sure didn't."

"I know," she said, then she laughed. He had never heard her laugh before. It was a warm, pleasing sound.

99

He turned and watched her. She raised her chin a little to do it, and the soft light washed through and over her taffy-coloured hair and around to the V in her throat. He flushed and looked out at the people moving aimlessly from fire to fire. There was something lacking. It took him a moment to understand it. The fear was gone. The breath of desolateness that had been shot through their other nightly camps. It sobered him.

"They'd do better to go to bed," he said. "There'll be plenty of nights they won't sleep. This is only the first brush with Indians we'll have."

"You'll talk them out of fighting us," she said softly.

He didn't give in to the desire to look around at her, so he shook his head facing forward. "Even if I could, I'm not sure your uncle's in favour of it, Melissa."

"Oh, he'll come to it. You'll see. I know him very well. He's had a hard life, Lew. Like my father; only he's younger. He always was a fighter."

He considered that for a time. "Most Mormons aren't," he said. "It used to make me disgusted, seeing how they'd let the night-riders burn 'em out and flog 'em, and all."

"You're wrong," she said. "They're all fighters. You'll see it, too. Back there, Lew, they didn't think fighting would help. They wanted to live in peace. That's why they were against men like you who fought back. Because they thought maybe the gentiles would come to their senses someday and remember."

"Remember what?"

"That our grandfathers came to this country so's we could all worship God according to our own lights, Lew."

"Well," he said tartly, "somewhere along the years folks've plumb forgot that."

"That's what I mean. The Saints've tried it one way. It didn't work. Now they're going out to make their own Promised Land where no gentiles will bother them, and after that—no gentiles had better bother them, either. You'll see."

"Is that what your uncle says?" He was looking steadily at her now.

She shook her head at him. "No. If it is, I don't know. That's what *I* say. I know our people. I know you, too."

He felt the strange stirrings rustling softly to life within him. He looked away from her and spoke gruffly. "Well, if you know me so well, then I reckon you know I'm sleepy and you'd better get back to your folks."

She went so obediently it made him feel ashamed for the second time in the same day. He lay back, shook up his covers, ground his teeth and groaned at himself, feeling meaner than ever.

Chapter Six

" ROLL 'EM !"

They rolled through the cold fall days into the spanking face of new-winter. They held to their course under cold grey skies and threatening gusts of icy sleet. They rocked along through prairie storms and corraled at night with frost on the nose-hairs of the animals and beards of the men. But they rolled.

The first pass had been the easiest, but by now they had scouts and Lew worked them like a well-rehearsed little army. He would study the mountains through the wintry blasts that came down at them, and send men to seek out passes where a skyline indicated a pass might be.

He came to rely more and more on big Danton Mills and powerful Caleb Bullard. There were others, like Charley Crawford—whose dislike of Lew seemed lost completely now. But the three of them, Lew, Cal, and Danton, were usually in a tight circle at night, mapping out the route ahead.

Elder Mortonson, as flinty, abrupt and solemn as ever, came often to council with Lew and his lieutenants. Cal was spending more of the evening hours with Mary Murphy. Lew noticed it without commenting, just as he noticed how Jakob would be watching him with his slow, steadily pained look, when he thought Lew didn't know.

The days were savage with only icy showings of sunlight that had no warmth, but the nights were bitter cold; worse than any they had known back in the 'States.

The afternoon of the last day of double-yoking up a particularly bad rise in the mountains was drawing to a close; the first prairie shadows were lengthening, wheeling faint and vast across the dying land. Nights fell swiftly now. There would be sickly, pleading light, then darkness. It happened that fast, and a man who walked ten feet out of the sunlight into the shadows would begin freezing instantly.

Elder Mortonson dropped down with mud on his boots and the callouses of his hands worn pink from labour. Lew had a tiny fire going. He and Danton and Caleb were hunched over it, still with weariness. Their fronts warmed quickly and their backs were freezing cold. None of them looked up at the leader. He spread his hands toward the little blaze.

"We are in the land of the Philistines," Mortonson said with weariness dripping from each word. "Zion lies beyond."

Lew was tempted to say something less symbolic, more pointed, but he didn't. He simply lifted his face and looked over at the big man, waiting. It was his way.

Mortonson spoke again. "The way is hard, the suffering great. We will win through."

Lew spoke that time. There was a little of the darkness of his spirit in the words. "Some of us, Elder. Some of us'll win through, like you say, but when we do, it'll be walkin', and maybe on frozen stumps at that."

Mortonson looked irately at him. His eyes were sunken and tired-looking beneath the edges of his tufted eyebrows. "What do you mean by that, Lewis?"

"I mean that if you don't pick a wintering spot pretty quick, the snow'll do it for you." Lew straightened up a little. Their eyes met and held. "If it was just the people, why I reckon we could send out hunters even this late in the year and freeze us up a lot of meat. Cut wood too, for that matter. But how're you going to keep these animals going on nothing but a diet of snow?"

Mortonson's gaze became a cold, fierce thing. He didn't speak for a long while, and in the meantime the other men were looking at him, waiting. "We'll rest across the last range. We'll rest when we're on the plains before Zion."

"The plains of Abraham," Caleb said softly, lowering his dark glance to the fire. "You won't make it."

Mortonson's glance flashed a hot fire at them all: "You are discouraged. We'll make it."

Lew contradicted him flatly, both with words and an aggressive shake of his head. "We won't. There's no way in God's world to cross those Colorados. The passes are ten feet deep in snow now. Oh, they'll thaw, I reckon, before real winter sets in—but we won't be close enough to 'em to get over in time."

"No?" Mortonson said. "They tell me the worst pass is less than sixty miles from us, right now."

"Sixty miles," Lew said shortly, "used to be two days' travel. Now it's three days' travel. We've got to hunt up a south-slope and set up a wintering camp. The oxen are about done for, an' the horses are no better."

Mortonson, contrary to the expectation of all three of them, didn't explode into his towering wrath—which had become more and more evident as the last thirty days had gone by and the strain ate into him. He didn't show the quick-running of dark blood under his face. He looked into the little fire and, if anything, some of his spirit seemed to evaporate.

"A man waits a long time for his hopes," he said in his deep way of speaking. "A long time. It is a heart-breaking thing to go uphill forever and never quite make your summit. Zion. We have been led out into the desert. We have left our dead behind—all we knew and all we had. We are persecuted people and the Promised Land isn't far. A man strives . . ."

Lew heard it all. He had heard it all before, many times. Not just out here in this godforsaken end of nowhere, with beetling mountains hanging out over them in black wrath and relentless defiance, but back in the sweet-water counties of his youth. In the far-away valleys with the tall graze and rich browse, the blood-and-gold sunsets, and within the low, thick-walled log houses of his kind, where the fires on the hearths burned cherry-red and low.

He fought against the blackness that came into his soul and saw how Danton and Caleb were lost in their own grey worlds. He raised his head and looked over at the big, shaggy patriarch. Mortonson was finished. There was only the soft soughing of the night chill through the trees near them to break the silence.

"I reckon," he said softly, "there isn't much in life a man doesn't have to struggle for. I think I'm made for struggle, and I don't fight it. I don't mind, Elder." There was a power of soft strength in his voice; in his glance and his lean, weathered face.

"But I don't think runnin' stubborn-blind headlong into disaster's the way to get over the mountains to the Promised Land, either. I think we've got to cache; got to find a place for wintering. Those passes are closed to the wagons. Even horsemen couldn't get through them. We've got to do like the Indians do. Fort up and pack our supplies and cut cottonwoods and brush and what grass is left, for the livestock. I know how you feel. Most of us feel the same way—I know I do. I want to get there, too, as bad as you do, I reckon, but I want to get there alive. I want to see all of us get there alive. Going stubborn into those snow passes won't get us anywhere but dead."

Lew looked back into the fire, saw its dying struggles,

fished around behind him for more ragged-ended tree limbs, and poked new life into the thing. No one spoke.

Mortonson sat for an hour that was a cramped, cold lifetime, then he got up and went out of their firelight. Lew looked after him. He saw the mighty proportions of the man. He saw the dismal, fitful fires of the people within the wagon circle beyond, huddled over as though seeking visions, Indian-fashion, in the little fires, then he looked at Danton and Caleb. Neither of them returned his look. They were absorbed, warmly hypnotised, by the blaze.

There was nothing else they could do. They all knew it, and one man's stubbornness had pushed them this far, otherwise they would have wintered weeks back. Lew watched the way people studied the leaden, skulking skies through eyes hindered by hoar-frost. He saw the gauntness come among the animals, the fast-growing weakness, and finally, after three more days of heart-breaking toil that netted the huge wagon train a miserly sixteen miles, he went through another night camp to the cooking fire of Elder and Jakob Mortonson.

He stood above them with the bluest pair of eyes in the encampment on his face. He knew she was watching him; it added to his anguish, for he had come to speak plainly. Elder Mortonson glanced up and their eyes locked. The older man spoke first.

"I know, Lewis. I know. It grieves a man—but I see it."

"Now, then," Lew said softly. "Right now—to-night. We're in a good tight valley. There's feed on the south slopes. We'll find no better place."

"How do you know?" Mortonson's eyes had a strange, quizzical look in them.

"Because I've had men scouting for the last two days. This is the best spot within twenty miles."

Mortonson dropped his head a little and shot a swift glance at his brother. Old Jakob was looking up at Lew, though. He had more weariness in his glance. There was only a spark of the old steel-flakiness left. He was worn out and looked it. He said nothing. Like his daughter, he looked up into the younger man's face and held his silence.

The Elder nodded his head several times and spoke without looking up. "All right, Lewis. It is God's will. Tomorrow use your scouts to make sure there are no savages about. Detail men for grazing the animals."

"There'll have to be hunters, too," Lew said quietly, looking at Melissa for the first time; seeing little of her in the frosty darkness but what the firelight showed him; it wasn't enough. "Hunters and guards and wood fellers and browse cutters. It's late, Elder—we'll have to work fast."

Mortonson nodded again. "Take the strongest and youngest men, Lewis," he said.

Lew entered into the organising with a thoughtfulness that was manifest. He sent out hunters under Caleb, whom he knew from their early years to be an expert hunter. He sent out men under Danton to forage browse for the lean animals, and he organised parties for grazing the animals. It was a hard undertaking for all of them. Lew spared only the very old among the people, and the very young. All others laboured, women and men and in-between children.

In the activity itself there was a certain spiritedness that lifted them up and made of their common plight a challenge. Lew kept it that way. Completely unknown to him was the word "morale," but in essence he sensed its value.

The winter came, finally, with a bone-breaking cold typical to the uplands. The Mormons staggered under loads of snow. They kept their tiny fires going and constantly thawed out their frozen boots and clothing. It was God's will, too, evidently, that it wasn't an unusual winter. The people from the middle central states suffered less than those from the places farther south, but the stock suffered the worst. When spring finally came, some beasts had died and none were able to do more than drag themselves to the

107

new feed; there was no strength in it, but there was nourishment of a sort, so that, while they sweated easily and were loose, at least they gathered an iota of new life into their chilled, sluggish hearts and fought to live a little longer.

When the sun finally came back to the north country with its precious warmth, the Mormon camp was a great meadow of scarecrows, both human and animal, and Lew sat down weakly with a thankfulness in him he couldn't quite express, even though he tried, with a head bent low under the starry vault at night.

But the days were still short and the animals weak, so they lay over into the warm times and let their animals grow strong again. Some, like Lew's black horse, being younger, more sturdy of build and soul, even got sleek and shed off so that their hides shone with health. It was then that Elder Mortonson came again to the fire of Caleb and Danton and Lew. He sat cross-legged and accepted a slab of rare elk steak from Caleb, eating into it with a fitting appetite.

"We'd best be moving, boys." He was speaking to them all, but his glance was for Lew alone. "The passes are open, they tell me."

"They're open," Lew said simply.

"Then we'd best be moving."

Lew nodded and smiled. It wasn't so much an effort as it was an unaccustomed expression. He felt the strangeness in his face. "We'll make it now. It won't take long."

"We've been cut off from the world for a long time," Danton said musingly. "Like being in prison."

Caleb ate and said nothing, but he listened, and when Mortonson left, he too arose and looked at his cousin and Danton Mills. "We've got a lot to be thankful for. I reckon I'll go over to the Murphy wagon." He went. Danton looked up slowly and followed the squat hulk of

Caleb Bullard with his head. There was a growing warmth in his face that hadn't been there in a long time.

"I reckon it's always like that, isn't it?"

Lew looked over at him, puzzled. "What?"

"That. Cal and the Murphy girl—you an' Melissa—someday me and someone, too. Life; that's what I was thinking about. Life goes on whether we're shut up here in these mountains or whether we're even alive at all. It keeps right on coming and going."

Lew was silent while he ate. He thought of Melissa. The winter had been hard on all of them, but she had been busy. There were serveral deaths among them. Five new births. Illnesses. She had been as busy as anyone. He hadn't seen her as much as he had the summer before. He stirred restlessly where he sat and fought against a desire to get up and go over to the Mortonson fire.

Danton Mills spoke without even looking up. He was sprawled out, full and satisfied and with a returning hopefulness in him—and a faint spark of his humour, too.

"Well, it's spring again. Directly there'll be colts and calves and—hell—why don't you just get up an' walk over there? She won't bite you, and you're bothering me, squirming around like that."

But Lew didn't go. He cleaned up their utensils and went out to look at his black horse. It was late, for the sun still hurried out of their valley and snatched away the wonderful warmth. He walked among the animals and saw how the females were swelling with young. How they all stood quiet and chewed their cuds and switched their tails and eyed him askance. They would be under harness and yoke and saddle soon.

He turned at the sound of her voice. It was something that filled in the hollow space within him.

"Hello."

"Hello, Melissa."

She looked filled out, too. The fullness had returned to

109

her face. The suppleness of her figure and the head-back way of going that she had, was there in the stillness, in the soft-fragrant wonder of the new life; the spring eventide. She was very beautiful, like that. With the old camp and the gaunt wagons as her background. With the wilderness far off, gloomy and inward looking, relieved by her fairness.

"You don't look very happy, Lew."

"I'm happy enough, ma'm." He looked out over the animals again with the great wave of peacefulness in him like a surfeiting wave of warmth. "I'm plumb happy. We'll be moving in the morning."

"It's been a hard winter, hasn't it?"

He looked back at her. "Yes, it was hard, Melissa. It could have been harder."

"I'm very proud of you, Lew."

He was surprised and rattled by the quiet, very direct, intent look she used with her statement. "Me? Why?"

"Lew, I wish there was a way for me to reach around behind that armour of yours."

"Armour? What're you talking about, Melissa?"

"Don't be disagreeable with me, Lew. You have an armour. It's something you've built up over the years. I reckon you had to, back home. It's sort of like a wild horse has. A way of defending himself; a kind of inwardness that won't let anyone get very close to him. You've used it to repel folks because of that curse you said you had. You don't want people to get too close to you, Lew. That's what I meant when I said your armour."

He fell into a silence, looking at her, wondering about her with a slight uneasiness. Feeling that she had Aunt Jem's way of seeing into a person. Right through them so that they held no secrets inviolate.

"That's why you won't let me explain why I'm proud of you. Because of your armour. As soon as I tell you that if you hadn't stopped my uncle when you did, he'd of driven us all to our deaths with his fanatical hurry to get to Zion, you'll belittle yourself. You'll brush what I'm saying aside because it's too close to the truth, and you don't want people to see good in you—be attracted to you. Well, you did it, anyway. You saved a lot of lives. You saved those men in the Missouri river, Lew. You saved more men, red and white, back where we met the Indians. Last winter you saved a lot of people by forcing my uncle to stop and winter. Maybe you even saved your own life and mine." She turned away from the drawn look of his face and looked at the drowsing animals around them with a sad thoughtfulness.

"So you see, Lew, that curse you had isn't in you any more. My uncle told you that and you walked away. Remember that night? I do. Well—he was very right. I tried to tell you that, too, and so did Caleb. I'm telling you again." She swung back swiftly and fastened her intent look on his face. "Has the winter changed you any? Has it made you think, Lew? Can't you see it like I do?"

Very gravely he reached out and put a hand on her shoulder. He didn't want to hurt her again; make himself feel mean, like he did whenever he rebuffed her. "Melissa; I reckon a person can be only half right sometimes."

"What do you mean?"

"Well, I don't figure I've been a saviour, only a helper. We all worked together."

"No," she said firmly, almost frowning at him. "You were the leader this last winter. We both know that; so does my uncle; so do the people. They respect you very much, Lew."

He held her shoulder and moved his arm a little so that he shook her slightly. It silenced her. but the intent look was still in her glance up at him.

"Listen, Melissa; I helped—you're half right. Maybe the curse isn't in me like you say—God, I hope so—time will tell. Let's let it go at that."

He dropped his hand and turned away from her. She stood back in the new grass watching his lean figure move out toward the old wagon circle.

He went slowly, knowing she was watching him. The soft pink of dusk came swiftly and brought a hint of chill over the high mountains with it, but there was a smell— almost a feel—of stirring, burgeoning life, new and vibrant and eager, in the gloaming. He went back into the circle and saw the people making their cooking fires. Without more than acknowledging a few calls, he turned and went over where Danton and Cal lay sprawled. Both looked up at him with impassive stares, said nothing and lowered their heads, waiting. It would be a vain wait, for Lew had nothing to say.

When the camp was quiet, he lay in the stillness, looking up into the mottled heavens. There was something about her—a man couldn't put his finger on it, but it was there— something . . . He rolled up on one side and tried to sleep. The peacefulness came like a deep, glowing fever, and went all through him.

He slept and awakened hours later to the tumult of the aroused camp. An air of something very like festivity was over everything. Even the beasts felt it and strained into their harness when the newly-tallow'd drovers' whips swung out overhead with their familiar loud cracking sounds.

Somewhere, far back, some men broke into a lilting song. Lew finished saddling up, toed into the stirrup and swung up. He lifted his arm high and let it drop. Danton, far ahead, over toward the pass out of their hidden valley, waved his hat. The exodus began, and Lew watched it with a full heart.

They had hardship right from the start, but nothing could daunt spirits fresh from their frozen fetters. They battled over the swollen streams and up the sheer faces of towering cliffs. They worked days at clearing out storm-strewn passes and hacking away at the tumbled wreckage of forests laid low by plunging floodwaters. The way was hard and unrelenting, but the faith and spirit, and strength, of the Mormons was a match for the worst of it; and in time they broke out of the cordillera and came again to an immense plain where the grass was knee high to a mounted man, waving with a beckoning nod to their sore-footed animals.

Here they made a camp long enough to set up a smithy, and the wilderness rang to a sound as foreign to its fastnesses as the ocean waves. The clangour of hammer and anvil and the wheeze of leather bellows. The horses were shod, and the oxen. Wagon tyres were reinforced and mended and wheels set into them so that the cooling iron's shrinkage would set them together tightly.

Here, too, Lew's scouts came upon signs of Indians again. Lew himself found the not-quite-dead fire where warriors had eaten. He dismounted among his scouts and felt of the cinders and looked up at Danton Mills significantly.

"They haven't been gone long."

Mills looked uneasy. Lew stood up and let his sombre glance roam over the forests around them. Caleb was chewing on a long stalk of grass when he spoke.

"Best make the wagon circle tighter again and set out more guards. We're strong, but up here I reckon they're strong, too."

They went back. Lew told Elder Mortonson what they had found. The leader nodded pleasantly. He had less fire and more patience in his glance now than he'd had the fall before.

"We'll set a closer guard, Lew. Could you figure out anything from the signs?"

"Only that they were Indians. Moccasin tracks around a-plenty."

"I reckon we'd best hurry up our mending and get under way again." Mortonson eyed the younger man steadily. "Lew—a man learns, doesn't he?"

113

Puzzled, but uneasy, too, Lew spoke as he turned away. "I reckon," he said, mounting.

They took two more days to strengthen their animals and vehicles against the scruff of mountains ahead, then they struck out once more. Lew rode ahead constantly now, for the places for ambushing were looming as their new valley, with its long, narrow plains, shrunk inward, eventually forcing the emigrants toward a heavily-timbered pass.

Lew called in his scouts. He was anxious, and with good reason. One Indian or a thousand Indians could hide in the primeval forest that lay athwart their pass, up ahead.

"Dan, I'm going to get every able-bodied man I can fetch back from the train. You and Caleb'll take half, and I'll take half. We'll sweep that forest on both sides in a body. It'll be bad if there're Indians in there, but it'll be worse if we don't do it. I like the looks of that spot the least of anything we've come through so far."

He went back, leaving his scouts clustered in the tall grass, waiting. When he found Elder Mortonson he called him aside and pointed out the place they'd pass through and explained the condition to him. Mortonson nodded accord and smiled. "Take who you want, Lew. I'll make up another guard of what's left. We'll roll 'em right through there behind you."

And that was how they worked it when the wagons finally got up to the frowning, perilous place. Lew swept the timbered slope to the south while the rest of the armed men under Cal and Danton Mills swept the northern slope. None of them saw an Indian.

Lew broke out into the next park and sat his horse with a steady look. His heart was beating raggedly and a bitter sense of triumph was in him, for there, not more than a mile ahead, riding at a long, loping gallop, obviously driven out of their hiding places by the overwhelming superiority of the Mormons, was a tawny band of painted warriors. He rode down into the open glade and swung down, stood hip-shot and smiling with a bleak look to his face, waiting.

The wagons came clumsily, rocking and settling and lurching over the uneven, rock-strewn pass. Horsemen came swifter, and Elder Mortonson rode down from the train almost before Danton and Cal came over from their side of the pass. Mortonson sat his horse with a forward lean to him.

"You figured it right, Lew. Good."

"There weren't enough of them in that band to do it, Elder."

Mortonson watched the Indians stop and turn back from a great distance. "No, and like the first ones we met, I allow they had a hundred more of their skulking heathen brothers hidden away some place."

Danton swung down, as did Caleb. They were both smiling as coldly, as threateningly, as Lew had been. "You're gettin' so's you can smell 'em."

Lew laughed shortly. "That wouldn't be hard, either, Dan. They've got a gamey smell all their own." He turned and watched the lumbering wagons coming out into the long grass. His eyes were sombre. "This makes a difference, in here."

Mortonson looked down. "How do you mean?"

"Those mountains all around us. As long as we can stay in the open place, I reckon we'll be safe enough, but if we ever have to night in one of those passes, or all strung out like, I wouldn't give a copper for the chances of a lot of us."

Cal grunted and plucked at a stalk of grass. "That's easy, Lew. We make it a point to camp in the open."

"I reckon," Lew said dryly. "As much as we can, anyway, but don't forget, Cal, there's a lot of miles of mountains ahead of us. There'll be times when I don't think we'll be able to do that. Those are the nights I'm thinking ahead to."

Elder Mortonson pointed one powerful arm. "Look; more of the heathen."

Lew looked as did the others. Indians were coming out of the trees far above and on both sides of the pass they'd just come through. Lew nodded and studied the little park they were in. It occurred to him to be thankful the grass was thick with juice or the Indians could have burned them out in the night. He estimated their numbers. They were far short of being strong enough to try a frontal assault on the Mormon train. He turned to the Elder. "I reckon we'd best have 'em all corral tight, right in this little meadow—don't you?"

Mortonson nodded without speaking, reined his horse over and headed back toward the lumbering behemoths that were spreading out in the park.

"Lew, how far you reckon we must be from Zion?"

Lew shrugged. "Have no idea, Cal. Go check the Elder's maps. I'd like to know myself. All I've gone by is what he's told me of the route. That and a compass Melissa gave me at Christmas, last." Caleb rode slowly back down the vale and Danton squatted on his heels and squinted out at the motionless cavalcade of savages.

"Looks like we won't talk our way past these, Lew. Look at them. They're riding back a little and unlimbering their bows."

Lew looked. The Indians were indeed coming closer. Some of them were making gestures intended to be both insulting and defiant. Others let out whoops that were redmen challenges to individual combat, but the Mormons didn't know it. They were smaller, more powerful and compact than the Utes had been. Also, they were quite obviously more aggressive than any other Indians the emigrants had come across to date. Lew waited until they stopped, then he stood up. Several of the warriors let off arching, high flying arrows that came down far short of where the Mormons stood. Lew looked around and saw Caleb's rifle.

"Cal? See—"

"Look! Here comes one—by the great horned spoon!"

A fighting buck was coming fast, straight at them. He was a side-rider, something they hadn't seen before. An Indian who rode hanging over the off side of his racing horse so as to present as small a human target as he could. He was emitting some kind of a high, shrill chant as he charged straight at the startled Mormons. Lew drew his pistol by instinct, too amazed for words. Caleb knelt and lifted his rifle. A man who had once "barked" squirrels on the top of the head in the rain forests back home, he was a deadly shot.

At the last possible moment, the warrior swerved his horse, swung his body upright and pulled his war bow back to his chin. At the precise moment, Caleb fired.

The sound made the horses of the Mormons start and snort, but the exulting hostile warrior's arrow went whistling far overhead. The Indian was knocked off his horse backwards, as though a mighty fist had struck him high on the chest. His horse stumbled, regained his balance and came to a bewildered, head-up stop. The silence held until Lew's black horse whinnied high and shrill. The Indian horse turned then, being closer to the smell of Mormon horses, and trotted over. He was roped easily.

From the distance came a great wail from the watching Indians. Lew holstered his gun and turned toward Caleb, who was still chewing his length of succulent grass. "Perfect, Cal."

The liquid dark eyes swung and held to Lew's face. There was an ironic mocking look to them. "Let's go see what I flushed."

The bulk of the men walked over to the Indian. He was dead, with a gaping hole in his chest. Danton Mills looked from the wound to Cal's rifle. "Cal—what you got 'er loaded with?"

Cal coloured a little. "Well, I had a hard time trading for the piece as it was, and then only got it because the other feller didn't have powder or shot. I've been begging up a little powder now an' then, but the best I could do for balls was some bolt heads from the mended wagon wheels."

Shocked, Lew looked away from the mess such a cartridge made. "Scalp's yours, Cal," he said. Several of the men laughed tightly at Cal's stunned expression.

"Now listen, Lew. A man'd eat dog'd scalp one, I reckon—but not me."

They left the Indian where he lay and went back to their horses. The wagons were corraling. Men's shouts came softly into the fading twilight as the drovers herded the loose-stock inside. Mounted, they rode back in a body. Drovers looked at them as they went past. Some called out banteringly. Children and women looked quickly up, and down again.

Lew went directly to the Mortonson wagon, where Melissa was building a little fire. He found their leader in deep conversation with several other men. Waiting, Lew bent down and helped Melissa with the fire. Neither of them spoke. It was awkward that way. Lew was looking at the girl, wondering, when Elder Mortonson came up and hunkered.

"You wanted me?"

"Only to find out about the guard, is all."

Mortonson's steely eyes glinted dully. "That's in your department from now on," he said. "That's what I've been talking over with the others." He paused a moment to let it sink in, then he held out a rumpled, soiled piece of paper.

"This'll give you the names of able-bodied men." He sat hunkered there with the hard little smile lurking behind his bold glance, saying nothing.

Lew took the paper and glanced at it briefly, unseeingly; then he flushed and straightened up. Elder Mortonson got up, too. He turned abruptly and walked back to where Jakob was standing, looking at Lew's profile with a solemn stare.

Melissa straightened up and walked a little closer to Lew. The smoke was rising swiftly, but its light was weak and futile against the fading sunlight. "Well," she said.

"Well, what?"

Her blue glance flashed testily at him. "Head of our scouts and now head of our defences. That's putting a lot of faith in one man, isn't it?"

He felt the irritation coming up and tried to stem it by saying nothing back to her. She wouldn't let it stop there, though.

"Lew, there's a lot to be learned from nursing people. Did you know that?"

"I've never nursed anyone, but I reckon there is. A person's bound to learn."

"Some will, and some won't," she said tartly. "You just plain won't."

He eyed her warmly. "Melissa, why do you go out of your way to rub me the wrong way?"

"That's what I'm talking about. Some people learn by nursing folks. I learned a lot about men from Cal when he was sick. I think I understand you better than you understand yourself."

"What's that got to do with always stabbing at me?"

"More than you think, Lew. It's your kind of medicine. I'm gambling on that, but I think I'm right."

"I don't understand you at all," he said flatly, coldly.

"A man divided within himself—that's you, Lew. You

don't want to believe what we all have told you. You just won't let yourself, is all."

He stood in silence, gazing into her face. The splashing sunlight, dying and red and brilliant, flashed over her taffy hair, making it soft and pastel. Her eyes reflected some of the saffron hues that came slamming back defiantly from the purpling mountains with their bristling coating of pines and firs.

"Melissa, there are times when I could shake you good," he said finally.

She didn't show any disapproval, just the level intentness that made him uncomfortable. "Anything else?" she asked with a low-voiced casualness that fooled him.

He started to move away. "I don't know," he said, walking over where men were watching them, waiting. "I'll be damned if I know what else I'd like to do to you."

Chapter Seven

The night was a sombre thing full of fear and dread.
Even Lew hated to see it come, and wished from a stric-
tured heart for it to stay. But it came, with its dark brood-
ingness, its awful, deep stillness, and he couldn't sleep, but
went constantly among the out-flung guards he had spaced
close enough together so that, by crouching, they could
sky-line and watch one another. He met Danton and Caleb
in the deepest part of the frightening hours. The three of
them were armed with revolvers and rifles and stood looking
into one another's faces with the same tightness up around
the eyes.

"I've heard it said they don't fight much at night."

Lew answered wryly. "I've heard that, too. I never
hoped it was true as much as I do right now."

"What about to-morrow?" Caleb asked. "I've been
through that pass across the valley. There's a lot more
trails before you can see to clear ground again."

"Can we make it to open land again by sundown to-
morrow night, Cal?" Lew was conscious of the earnestness
in his own voice.

Cal sounded doubtful. "I don't see how, Lew. These
days are awful short now. There's a lot of dead-falls to
be broken up and hauled out of the way."

Danton spoke low, as though the night oppressed his

121

spirit. It did. "We could send on pioneers, Lew. Men and oxen to work fast.

"And a body of armed men ahead of them, or with them," Cad added hopefully. "That way—if we worked hard and fast—we might make it."

"Then we'll do it like that," Lew said, "but unless I'm as wrong as wrong can get, we'll have fighting with them to-morrow."

He left them after that, and walked among the guards. They were changing on the hour. Men came and went through the dew-drenched grass; some, thinking they were far enough from the women and children and elders, cursed low and to themselves.

The night was a harrowing thing full of shadows and terror. It seemed to last for ever, to Lew. He didn't close his eyes until he could see a little of the new day insinuating itself under the bulbous belly of the heavy darkness, between the sky and a mountain top. Then he climbed high onto a Conestoga wagon-box and looked out over the glade. If there were Indians out there—and he didn't doubt it at all—they weren't close.

He smelled the freshness, the crisp dewiness of the new day, and sank down on the high, hard seat, and let the rifle he held sag in his grip. A lassitude almost like a sickness stole into him. Reaction. Taut nerves drawn up like bow-strings, relaxing all at once. It made his flesh crawl. With a low growl he swung down from the high perch and walked through the damp grass, making a complete circle of the wagons to wear away the strain a little, then he ducked under a long tongue with an ox-yoke tossed over it hap-hazardly, and came back into the circle. People were moving slugglishly in the chill. He watched them from eyes that grated in their sockets, then he went toward his own pallet and was almost there when he heard it.

Suddenly, growing with the silence, a part of it but only

for a short while, a low insistent rhythm began to trouble the cold air. It grew louder, slowly louder; louder; it beat up into a thundering tramp, a muted, off-key sound of many horses coming at top speed. He ripped out a curse, snatched up the rifle and let out a long yell.

The effect was instantaneous, as though the Mormons had all been crouched impatiently, waiting for this signal. They tumbled out, clothed and half-clothed, and hardly clothed at all. Their hands gripped guns and shot pouches and powder flasks. Lew was running when he saw them making toward the side of the wagon circle, where the rolling thunder of the charging horsemen came from. He hurdled a drooping wagon-tongue and ran out where he could see them.

His guards were falling back slowly. Closing up and falling back on the wagon circle. He shouted at them to hurry. The men within the circle dared not fire so long as their companions were between them and the riders. It was the Indians.

Lew felt like taunting them, for, had they struck in the darkness, their chances of breaching the circle would have been immeasurably better. He watched them come down the little valley with their hair-raising screams that seemed to come straight from wild, maddened hearts. It was a head-on attack. There must have been a hundred or better of them, all riding like the wind, fanned out and howling like wild men, making the new day hideous with their noise.

He shouted until his throat was raw, and finally the guards saw their peril and ducked low, scooting for cover. Then the barricaded Mormons let off their first concerted volley. It was a long way for their guns, but it had an effect on the savages, if not with any carnage, at least with the noise that drowned out their own screams. Several of the Indian bands split off and rode as though to go down one side of the wagon circle, while the balance of them came on as they had before, only now there was less shouting and more determination in the way they levelled their bows and leaned low over their horses.

Lew clambered back inside the circle and watched his men crawling out from under the wagons, emerging among their friends. He knelt then, and waited.

The noise arose again and his heart beat a savage tattoo with it. Waiting; squatting behind meagre cover and waiting. A man flung himself down beside him. It was Cal. At that instant one of the split-off bands swept by letting off a lethal barrage of stubby war arrows. Cal ducked low, as did Lew, then they both came back up, picked an Indian, tracked him for a second and fired.

One of the hostiles went off sideways, pinwheeling. The one Lew shot at bent far forward and grabbed gaspingly for his horse's mane. He missed and went head over heels. The white men both bent to the re-loading. Sweat stood out on their faces. A fierce exultation showed in their eyes.

Other Indians were streaming past. An arrow struck the water cask on the side of the wagon where Lew was. He could hear the thing when it smashed into the curved oak. It made a solid, smashing sound. He threw up his rifle again. A big savage with his face painted in a series of saw-toothed designs came flashing by. Over the tautness of his bow both Lew and Cal could see the wild, black eyes. They fired almost in unison, the three of them. The Indian disappeared before their eyes and a quivering arrow buried its head and broke its shaft under the impact in the bed of the wagon that Cal had rolled behind the instant he fired.

Lew could see the Indian clearly in the crushed grass. He turned with a wild look and watched Caleb get back to his knees. "Are you still using bolt heads? Because if you are I might as well let you handle 'em single-handed. That one's just about blown in two."

Cal was re-loading, with his head down and the floppy brim of his cast-off hat shielding his face. When he looked up he had an almost gentle smile on his face. "Better'n eatin' dog," he said calmly, then turned back to the battle.

The sounds around them were diminishing. Lew canted his head, listening. Very slowly he got to his feet and looked around at the water cask. "I reckon that's the answer to what they wanted to know, Cal."

"What?"

"If we had enough guns to go around and knew how to use 'em."

Cal stood up and gazed at the dead Indian with the saw-tooth designs on his face. "'Pears to me it's a mighty expensive way of finding out," he said.

Danton Mills and Elder Mortonson came down the line to them. The Mormon Elder held a long Pennsylvania rifle with a maple stock in his big right fist. His hair was wild-looking, to match the shine of his eyes. Danton saw the dead Indian, went over to the wagon tongue and knelt on it, peering out into the grass. Very slowly, with a shocked look, he levelled a glance at Caleb.

"Let's see if we can't find you some rifle balls."

Elder Mortonson put his rifle butt down and leaned on it. "Lewis, there was no sense to the thing they did. They went right on by."

"I reckon they did—and fast. I think, though, all they wanted to do was test us."

Mortonson looked glum and tired. "They found out all they wanted to know then."

"But how many of us were hit?"

Mortonson straightened up a little. "I saw one dead dog, but there must be more damage than that. Melissa'll know. Let's go find her."

They walked up through the turmoil and saw men working with oxen and horses with arrow shafts sticking out of them. Small, hushed words of profanity came to them. The Elder, his face set in stern disapproval, said nothing nor looked around to see who swore. They found Melissa climbing down from a freighter's wagon with high side-boards. She took Lew's offered hand and made the last jump, then brushed back her hair and looked inquiringly from one to the other.

"How many were hurt, Missy?" Elder Mortonson's drumroll voice was all but lost in the bedlam.

"Four men and a little boy. None of them look to be seriously hurt, though. The little boy was shot in the side of the head. The arrow tore his cheek and took off the lobe of his ear. The men are wounded in the arms and legs. None very bad." She swung her glance to Lew. "How many of the devils did you get?"

He was startled at the fierceness in her look. "Couple, ma'am. I don't suppose altogether there were many of them shot. A moving man's hard to hit."

"Caleb all right?"

"Right as rain."

"Then send him up here to me, Lew. He has a gentleness to him, as a nurse." She swung away from them. Both of them watched her go, and were still standing there when old Jakob Mortonson came up with his face smudged and puffy-eyed.

"Sure came fast. I barely had time to get set." His wan eyes went from face to face, then dropped away. Lew was watching the people making their morning cooking fires. His body felt emptied of all strength and energy. He looked at Elder Mortonson.

"I reckon we'd better roll 'em. They can eat parched corn and meatlings on the way. We've got to get through the passes up ahead before sundown. And you'd best go out with a lot of pioneers and oxen, chains and axes. Caleb'll show you the way and what to do. Take all the riflemen you can spare from the wagons—although I don't expect the red devils'll be able to circle around and get back up there that fast."

Mortonson listened with a nodding head. "You going to rest some?"

"Some," Lew said laconically. "All day if I can." He started down the circle for the spot where his bedding was. Danton Mills caught him in mid-stride and held his arm while he pointed toward a wagon.

"I tossed your beddin' in that one, Lew. Cal and I'll take over for to-day."

Lew veered off without a word for the wagon Danton had indicated. He climbed over the tailgate and got a wide smile from a fierce-looking man with a black, bristling beard, and dropped down onto his coverlets, shoved the rifle to one side, kicked off his boots and lay back. He was asleep almost before he closed his eyes, and all the shouting, jolting and lurching in Kingdom Come wouldn't have awakened him.

Danton mustered the riflemen, fifty strong and well mounted. He led them out ahead of the great line of wagons, leaving outriders on each side and flank of the train, with a full umbrella of protection.

Elder Mortonson and Caleb Bullard led the pioneers with their yokes of oxen and their great chains dragging, straight up into the passes ahead. Danton fanned his men out and swept through the forests on either side and back again. There were no Indians and no one really expected there to be, but all day long the men laboured with sweat pouring and lungs heaving. They no sooner cleared one place out wide enough for the wagons than they had to go ahead to another.

After six hours of it, Elder Mortonson sent back the first group and had the second relay sent in. They worked without respite. Without food and with only water to keep them going, and when they finished it was very late, but on the far side of the gnawed, blasted and torn-out pass, lay a desert so vast it dwarfed the mightiest wagon and the largest ego among them. Beyond that great, dead land, the sun was sinking low.

Drovers hurled their animals into the pass and over it and into the next. They kept the wheels rolling, and the sound of their whips making a constant sound like a battle being fought in the near distance. The animals were shaking with fatigue and willing to stand wide-legged and exhausted, when they were all out into the open country again. Caleb rode his horse back down the line several times, encouraging the men and animals. He had a personal stake in what they were accomplishing. Vindication came grudgingly, but it came.

Elder Mortonson sat his horse beside Jakob and Melissa, and watched the last vehicle stagger and lurch over the pass and debouch out onto the desert, then he bent his head in the gloaming and prayed.

When Lew awoke it was broad daylight again and men were hazing the stock back toward the foothills already. He sat up and looked out at the staggering land mass westward. His eyes burned, and he was fiercely hungry. He dressed by putting his boots back on, and his hat; then he went over the side of the wagon and around to where a water cask hung with a shred of grey linen beside it. There had been no soap for two months. Not since early spring.

He washed and felt better, smelt the cooking fires and went around among the wagons—and ran into Melissa. She looked twice at him, and shook her head.

"You're a total mess."

More appalled at her frankness than indignant, he squinted up his sore eyes and looked down his nose at her. "Do you reckon you're a real beauty, ma'm?"

"You tell me that," she said, giving him look for look.

But he shied away from the subject. "I'm sort of hungry. Do you reckon there's someone hereabouts hasn't put up their meat yet?"

"I reckon," she mocked him. "Come on; I'm making coffee and antelope steaks for my hospital."

He followed her dutifully and was fed. She kept up a running conversation while she worked, and he rarely answered. Then Caleb came up and dropped down red-eyed and exhausted. His liquid-dark eyes swept up to Melissa's face with a weary little smile. "Can you feed well men, too, Missy?"

She laughed in his face and looked over across the compound. Lew turned. A sturdy, tall girl was beckoning with exaggerated motions. Lew didn't recognise her right away. Not until she put her hands on her hips and cocked her dark head to one side; then he did.

Turning, he beat Melissa to it by nudging Caleb. "There's a woman over there using sign language to you, Cal. I reckon she's a better cook'n Melissa is, anyway."

He said it so soberly, so absolutely devoid of any expression and without looking up from his plate of food, that the stillness settled down around him almost unnoticed. When Caleb left and Lew raised his eyes, he was shocked at the look of her. It was more than just indignation, which he'd expected; it was anger of a kind he'd never seen in her before. Mortonson anger; full-bodied and savage. There was a deep, twisted hurt in her eyes, too, and he wanted to swear at himself. What he'd meant for dry humour had turned into the most awful debacle he'd ever caused.

Very slowly he laid his plate aside and got up. "Melissa, that was supposed to be funny. I'm powerful damned sorry, ma'm." Beyond that he couldn't find the words to go on, so he stood there like a stone.

And she finally spoke. All that she said he didn't remember, but enough of it stayed to make him white in the face. Scorching, deep-hurting words. Bluntness with dagger points. Harshness that raked and scourged him and blasted him for a blind fool, a man with a warped soul, a savage, and worse. When it was all over, she swung away and almost ran from him. He still stood there with the shock in his face when Danton Mills came up.

"Lew, Elder wants you over by the first wagon." Lew didn't move. Danton looked at him queerly and repeated it. That time Lew turned stonily and walked away. Danton's perplexed gaze followed him. He, too, was still standing over the barely-touched food when Melissa came down out of her hospital wagon, walked over beside Danton and watched the retreating figure of Lew Landsborough.

"Danton? Do you like him—really, I mean?"

Danton's perplexity came up anew. "Like him? I reckon we all like him. Don't you?"

She was slow answering. "Sometimes, yes. Sometimes he makes me furious. I don't know whether I can keep it up or not."

"Keep what up?"

She looked up at the big man. There was a warmth of dry tears in the glaze of her glance. "Playing a part with him. Being something I'm not."

Danton sank down beside the little fire and very deliberately lifted the plate Lew had set aside. "I'm big and dumb, Melissa. Right now I'm too tired to care and too hungry to worry—but if you want to sit down here and talk while I'm eating, I'll listen."

She sat down on the ground and didn't even look at him. Hardly knew he was there at all. "He's as sick in his way as Caleb was in his. It's been a fight for over half a year, Danton, trying to cure him. He's stubborn—like a bull. I'm trying to make him see that he *isn't* cursed with that —that—power for destroying people that he thinks is in him. Danton, he *isn't!*" She flung the word out so that Danton looked up quickly at her. Soothingly he spoke around a great gorge of food.

"Of course he isn't, Missy; we all know that."

"But he doesn't believe it, and that's why I'm acting a

part. I'm shadowing him all the time, talking to him, trying to break down the barrier he has inside him."

"Well," Danton said soberly, "wouldn't it be better if you just let nature take its course, Melissa?"

"How? Tell me how and I'll do it."

"Don't work at him so hard. Let him come out of it by himself."

"He'll never do it, Danton. I don't believe anything'll ever do that for him."

Danton went on eating. He chewed with slow, rolling motions like a ruminating cow. Once he lifted his eyes and glanced over where Lew had gone. The ruminating stopped. He didn't move. Melissa saw and followed his stare.

Lew was talking wildly, using his arms. His eyes shone with a cold light and his fists were clenched. Elder Mortonson and Caleb were there. So was Jakob Mortonson and Charley Crawford, and a huddle of other men.

"I've got to ride down there. If I don't, they'll come up here."

"Lew," the Elder said in his deep, throbbing voice, "they don't even know *any* of us are up here yet. It was our scouts saw *them*. Their outriders haven't even tried to circle up this far toward the mountains. I don't allow they will. We'll just stay up here for a spell, and they'll go on by. Soldiers out here don't mean anything more'n that hostiles are running loose. Now we'll just wait over a day or two—we all need the rest, and so do our critters. They'll go on—"

"Don't be a fool," Lew said angrily. "You're jeopardising all the people because of one man. You almost did the same thing back on the Missouri. I'm going down there." He swung away from them. No one made a move to stop him.

Danton Mills walked up to the group and Caleb caught his arm, drew him to one side and told him about the soldiers the scouts had seen down on the desert far off, paralleling the Mormon encampment. Danton looked puzzled. "Where's Lew going? To tell them about those Indians that rode down on us?"

"No! He's going to give himself up to them. He says he'll endanger all of us if he stays here and lets them find him. It's that old idea of—"

"I know," Danton said, squinting after the retreating figure on the black horse. Then he filled his powerful chest with a mighty inhalation and let the air out with a hissing sound. "Cal, round up the scouts."

"What are you thinking about, Dan?"

"We'll go down there and tell that Army such a whopper of a lie about him being crazy we'll burn forever in hell for it. Hurry up, will you? I'll get a fresh horse."

Elder Mortonson came over stony-eyed when Danton rode up on his horse moments later. "What are you going to do?"

Danton glanced at the men riding toward them. He counted them in his anxious way, then he answered the Mormon leader. "Ride after him. Fetch him back, if we can. If we can't—if he gets to the Army first—why, then, I reckon we'll just have to make out like he's deranged from the wintering." Mills dropped his glance and beheld the hardness of the Elder's face. "What else can we do?"

"We'll all go," Mortonson said. "I'll get the men."

Caleb was hauling in beside Danton. He shook his head at the Elder. "You can't do that. Those savages are behind us somewhere. The wagon train's the most important thing. The people."

Danton Mills nodded his head. "That's right. Besides, if we took every Saint we still wouldn't have enough men to fight the Army—we wouldn't do that, anyway."

Elder Mortonson looked from one face to the other. Caleb was watching the distant speck that was a man on a black horse. He fidgeted and lifted his reins a little in impatience. "Let's go, Dan. He's making good time."

Mills shot Elder Mortonson a harassed look, spun his horse and gestured to the men behind them. They went out of the camp and down the slight incline to the edge ot the long, drab roll of desert that was spread out before them as far as they could see.

Caleb took the lead. He rode with his eyes fixed on Lew. Except for that one moving object, there was no sign of activity as far as any of them could see. Once, miles out into the warm sink, he twisted and looked back. No wonder the Army's scouts hadn't seen the Mormon wagon train. Even as close as five miles away, Cal himself had trouble making it out against the dark growth that was behind it.

He let his gaze come back to the men behind him. Fifteen of them. The core of Lew's guard unit. He saw Danton Mills looking at him and inclined his head a little. The big man reined over without breaking the stride of his horse.

"Where *is* this Army; do you know?"

"Not exactly. I've been watching Lew. If he doesn't find it, so much the better. If he does . . ." Danton let it trail off.

Cal lifted his glance to the distances again. Lew looked no closer than when they'd started out. He eased forward a little in his saddle. "Let's make some speed, Dan. If we lose him, we'll have to fall back on trackin', and that's powerful slow."

They spurred their horses into renewed effort and held them to it. The land fell away all around them. They were tiny, dark specks moving across a firmament **devoid** of anything save occasional scrubby growth that was greening a little. Colourless brush with spines and a stubborn, grizzled look to it.

133

Once in a while, as they rode, there were long, thin patches of white that were like unhealing wounds against the drab, lifelessness of the dun-coloured ground. The sun would hit those patches of alkali and reflect upwards, making the Mormon riders flinch and narrow their eyes from the sharp sting of glaring light.

Lew was far ahead of them and didn't appear to turn back and look, for he didn't alter his course at all, but headed down into the broadest part of the vast plain.

Caleb watched him with a wondering look. Once, he lowered his own glance and studied the packed earth they were riding over, then he grunted to himself. Lew was following the tracks of the Mormon scouts. That was how he was tracking the Army. Danton swore so suddenly it jarred Caleb out of his reverie. He looked swiftly at the larger man.

"There; behind us."

Caleb turned. Several of the scouts were riding twisted in their saddles, too. It was a lone horseman streaking toward them on a powerful chestnut horse. "Melissa!"

Danton looked more angry than disturbed. "I'll take the boys and ride on. You go back and make her get out of here."

Caleb's brow lowered. He looked quickly ahead and saw that they were gaining on Lew. He could even make out the details of his cousin and the black horse now. To stop now, to turn back for any reason, was gall. "No; let her come. When we catch him, maybe she might even be able to talk to the fool. There's no danger, anyway."

Danton swung and glared back at the girl again before he spoke. His agreement was in the annoyed shrug he made more than in his words. "She can't do any harm, I reckon."

They looked at one another, then Danton smiled crookedly. Cal returned the wry look. Neither of them spoke of the girl again, and only occasionally looked back. She was steadily gaining on them. Her chestnut horse was surprisingly strong and willing.

Then Lew stopped. Caleb saw it first and called out to Danton. The big man squinted at the distant figure. Lew had turned. He was watching them. They couldn't see anything of his expression, but both of them imagined how his eyes would look, and his stormy, stubborn jaw. They kept right on riding, a little surprised that Lew sat there as long as he did. Caleb understood the reason first.

"He's seen Melissa."

"Good; maybe he'll hold up."

But he didn't. The black horse flicked his tail. He had been spurred. Lew went over across the dead world again, only this time he was angling a little south. Danton unfurled a banner of staccato profanity that shocked Cal. His face was beet-red in wrath. "We can't push the horses like this all day, Cal."

They slowed and listened to the gusty breathing of their mounts. Danton watched Lew loping easily ahead. He leaned in his saddle as though to bridge the distance. "That black's more horse than I took him to be."

"He's all horse," Cal said quietly. "He's kept Lew ahead of better pursuit than we're offering."

They watched Lew draw away; then, to their relief, the pursued man slowed to a fast walk, too. Charley Crawford kneed his mount up beside the others. His nasal twang was particularly unpleasant in the steeped stillness of the desert.

"We could split up, boys, an' maybe cut him off. Ye'd think that danged horse'd be give out by now."

Cal considered it, then shook his head. "It'd make twice as much riding, Charley. He'd see us at it, too. He knows we're after him by now."

"Yeh," Danton Mills said gloomily. "All he'd have to do is ride in a straight line and all the surrounds we could make wouldn't put us any closer."

They rode knee to knee steadily, glumly, until a dark sorrel flash swung up beside them. Cal looked over into the flashing blue eyes.

"Missy, why didn't you stay at the wagons? No sense in you comin' down here. We'll fetch him back."

"Will you?" she said. "Not the way you're going now you won't."

Danton Mills bit down hard to keep from flaring back at the girl. He swung his head slowly and regarded her with a wooden, hostile expression. "Can you catch him?" he asked dourly.

"We won't have to," Melissa said. "That's why I rode after you."

Caleb looked up and didn't let her go on. "What are you talking about, Missy?"

"Indians, Cal. They came back."

Danton and Caleb hauled up so suddenly the men behind were slammed into them. For a second there was a tumble of horses and men and the loud, crashing voice of Danton Mills shouting at her over the scramble and cursing.

"What Indians? Back at the wagons?" He was turning his horse when he said it, eyes bright and full of horror.

"No, not at the wagons. They are the same ones. Look, you can see their dust." She pointed with a slim arm. Her hair was flying in wisps despite the ribbon she had hastily bound it behind her head with. Her bosom rose and fell and her face was flushed.

They could see the dust, south of them, a long way off. A great, dun-brown spiral of it churned to life under the hooves of hard-riding horsemen. Their attention had been so completely riveted on Lew that none of them had noticed it before.

"That might be the Army," Cal said rapidly, his nostrils quivering under the tension that gripped him.

Melissa turned with a fiery look. "It isn't. We saw

136

them back at the wagons. That's why I came after you. It's the same band. We saw them above us in the hills, but they must have decided we were too strong, corraled and all."

"They came back," Danton said harshly.

Melissa glanced at him swiftly. "They probably thought they'd catch us in the passes. They came through the hills spread out. We are corraled out on the desert, but from up there they must have seen the soldiers. We could hear them shouting to one another, then they swung south and went racing out over the desert. We saw it all."

"Look!" Caleb was pointing. "Lew's stopped."

They could see him sitting stiffly erect, head high and cocked a little. Melissa shot an imploring glance at Caleb and Danton. "Go back. I'll bring Lew."

Caleb shook his head and gathered his reins. He spoke without looking at the girl. "Dan, take her back with you. Leave me two of the scouts and take the rest of them back. There may be more savages in the hills."

" What're you going to do?"

" He's my cousin." Caleb didn't wait. He sunk in his spurs and raced overland toward the still, motionless figure far ahead that hadn't moved.

The distance closed rapidly, but by the time Caleb got close enough for Lew to hear him coming, his horse was beginning to falter in its stride. Lew turned and watched him come. He noted the condition of Caleb's horse and frowned. There was a faint, rippling sound of gunfire far off. By the time Cal was close enough to haul up, they could both hear it plainly.

" Lew, come on back. The Indians came back to the wagons."

The tortured blue eyes held to the dark, liquid ones. " Are they attacking?"

"No. Melissa rode after us. She said they came up on

those hills in back of the wagons and saw us forted up. She said they must've seen the Army from up there, too, because they lit out south, riding like the devil."

Lew turned his head back a little, sideways. His eyes had a faraway look in them; a misty, veiled, abstract appearance. "That's what it is. I thought it might be. They've hit the Army sure as shooting."

Cal got off his horse and loosened the cincha and stood there looking up at his cousin. There was a strained sardonic look to his face. "I reckon you'll say your special curse caused *that,* now."

Lew didn't answer him. He sat there like a statue. The black horse was breathing almost normally again but his sleek hide shone with sweat. The sun was warm, almost hot, and a tiny ruffled zephyr stirred at knee level, coming toward them with the insistent sounds of battle riding it like a series of soft coughs.

When Lew spoke again, it was with his old, quiet way of speaking. The way he gave orders and said things he'd thought over before he let them out.

"Cal; go back and get as many men as Elder Mortonson reckons he can spare from the defence of the wagon train. Have 'em bring every damned gun they can pack. If there's food handy have 'em fetch that too, but don't waste time with it. No oldsters and no youngsters, Cal. Have them line out along the fringe where the hills and the desert meet. They'll be backgrounded that way. Indian sentries—if they've got any—won't see 'em so quickly that way. Ride south with 'em, Cal. Due south until you can hear the shooting real good, then swing west." Lew stopped and looked down at his cousin. "Don't kill that horse going back, but push him to the limit. Go on."

Cal swung up, tugged at the latigo and tightened it sitting sideways as he did it. "What're you going to do, Lew?"

"Ride south from here. I'll keep a watch for you and you have a scout for me riding down the land a little. I'll wait when I think I'm close enough. You boys come down where I am when you see me." His unpleasant glance lighted with a little of the old fire and pain and defiance.

"Those redskins want a fight—why, I reckon we can oblige 'em."

Cal was turning his horse when Lew called out to him: "Cal? One more thing. If you have to chain Melissa to a wagon-tongue, don't let her follow you this time! Ride for it; I'll see you later."

Chapter Eight

The fierceness, the darkness of his harried soul, the anger
burning like a brush fire, rode with Lew on his big black
horse. The lust to fight was rattling loose in him. A surge
of anger founded in overpowering resentment that he had
been balked in surrendering himself. Because of stinking
wild men on stolen horses a-drape with clothing from
arrow-bristling corpses they had left in countless cabin
yards in this raw country.

Balked, he rode south, hearing the tumult of the rattling
gunshots and after a few miles, he could even hear the
screams of the savages ringing like bells in a tempest, dis-
organised, wild and uncontrolled. His eyes were partly
closed against the outpouring of the raw distances. There
was a writhing dust cloud off on his left a little. He swung
the black horse so as to be above the battlefield. He had
no desire to be down country.

Closer still, he saw them. Small specks in the dead
immensity. Some were a-horseback riding furiously as
though a horse wasn't something of flesh and blood and
lungs. Killing their animals heedlessly in their froth of
blood-madness. It made his rage course within him like
a steady fire.

He rode still closer and reined up. Now, the bedlam
was deafening. He could see the soldiers down, forted up

behind their horses. It appalled him because he'd been sure this would be the Army. Army always meant a lot of soldiers. Hundreds of them. Back home, when they'd come to stamp out the flare-ups against the Saints, they'd come a-riding with the metal clanking of them going on far ahead. And strong. Hundreds strong.

This was far away. Maybe the government didn't send out big armies. He shook his head to clear away the headlong rush of disconnected thoughts. Whatever the reason, that Army down there and off a little to his right, was down. It was forted up and fighting on its belly. There was a listing pole with a little pennant hanging from it and there were dark, motionless specks that would be dead soldiers. He turned and looked higher. Up along the foothills that were dim and shimmering with the warmth, on his left. Nothing. He turned the black horse and rode slowly up toward the hills. When he saw them they were still a long way off and by that time his resentment was seething so that it showed very cruelly in his face.

There was one rider loping easily toward him, down into the desert a mile or so from the brooding hills that back-grounded the rest of the Mormons. He reined up and waited, looking past the out-rider to the main body of men. Elder Mortonson must have just about stripped the wagon train. The men were bunched up so it was impossible to tell how many there were, but there were a lot of them. He could tell that without effort.

" Lew !"

It was Caleb again. He was riding Melissa's big chestnut horse. He watched his cousin come closer and saw where two pistol butts jutted up arrogantly out of his waistband and the long rifle was across his lap. He wondered grimly if Caleb had a pouch full of those bolt heads.

" Lew, it looks like they got the Army down out there."

" They have. Got 'em forted up behind their horses."

" God !"

Startled, Lew looked closely at Caleb. His cousin's dark eyes were wide and shocked looking. Lew twisted his features into a calm and bitter smile.

" Armies we're used to are a lot bigger, Cal. Maybe this is only a little bunch of soldiers." He swung back and studied the battlefield again, then just as calmly, turned and watched the Mormons. With a slow, almost lazy movement, he took off his hat and flagged with it. Instantly there were dozens of answering waves. He put the hat on again and ran his angry, flinty glance along the hills and the desert. " There's no way to surprise them that I can see, Cal."

" No; I reckon not. They're too far out from the hills."

" That's right. About the best we can do is split up and—" he stopped there, feeling the anger turn to slyness. " No, wait a minute. They want a fight, damn their heathen souls—well—we'll fix 'em good." He turned and waited until the small army of Mormons came thundering up. There were over a hundred of them. He nodded to Danton Mills and showed a wolfish smile to the others.

" Dan; take about seventy-five of those men and go back along the foothills. Have horse guards hide your critters. Station your men back in those trees and behind every clump of brush—then wait. Keep your eyes open and your guns ready—and wait."

" For what?" Danton asked.

Lew smiled wider at him. The same bleak, ugly, wolfish smile. " Cal and I'll take the rest of your men and go down there and get into the fight. We'll be out-numbered but at least we'll be astride. The soldiers are afoot. If the Indians think like I hope they do, they'll leave off fighting the soldiers long enough to tackle us. When they do we'll streak it for the hills and lead 'em into your rifle range."

Danton Mills' eyes were moving nervously from Lew's

face to the battlefield. He nodded grudgingly. "All right, but why don't we just sail out there and whip the hell out of them?"

"Because they'll run off. You saw how they fight, yesterday. We want to give them a fight and make it decisive. We'll never do it chasing them in country they know better'n we do. Go on, Dan." Lew turned toward Cal. "Pick out our men and let's go."

He turned and rode slowly away from them. Danton and Caleb called names. Their voices sounded like rolling thunder. Men split off and in their feverish haste they pounded after their leaders only half waiting to be called. When Lew turned and saw Caleb urging his horse ahead he called out to him.

"Walk him, Cal. Walk your horses. Those Indians've been using theirs just about to the limit. We'll need horse flesh later, save it now."

They walked all the way, until the wild screams of the redmen ripped into the gunfire and the staccato sounds lessened long enough for the embattled soldiers to look behind them. Lew heard their wild shouts and ignored them. He rode with his pistol in his right hand, his reins in his left, and his slitted eyes on the careening Indians. It was a strange way to enter battle. The Indians noticed it and drew off a little, gauging their new enemies, then they raised the yell again and whirled to face the mounted Mormons. Lew's voice rang clearly over the shouts.

"Give 'em hell, boys, but stay close together. Don't let 'em split us up. Fight on your horses. Don't dismount. Watch me—when I start to fall back on the hills, you do the same. Use your horses then. Save 'em all you can."

He had no time to say more. The Indians swirled away from the downed troopers and hurled themselves at the slowly advancing Mormons. Guns began to thunder among the thin line of riders. Lew turned quickly and looked at Cal. His cousin had his long rifle poised at his shoulder.

Lew's cold smile was strong. He lifted his hand-gun and let it ride. There was an iciness in him that was completely contrary to the tumult he was riding into.

The Indians were strong. They had losses; Lew could see where dead savages lay among their fantastically painted and braided horses, but the redmen were still over a hundred strong.

It was an unnerving sight the way they came straight at the Mormons. Lew reined up and his men stopped too. He held his breath for a fraction of a second, raised his pistol and aimed at a buck he thought was well within range—and fired. As though awaiting Lew's signal, the Mormon line of riders let off a crashing volley and were wreathed, almost hidden, in the pungent smoke. When it cleared the horses were plunging wildly but the Indians were reeling.

Almost before Lew could get set again a burly Indian stripped to g-string and moccasins rode around his shattered companions, screamed something in a piercing voice and rallied the warriors. They followed the man. Lew cursed to himself. The riflemen wouldn't have time to reload.

He swung and saw his cousin drop his long rifle and snatch a big dragoon pistol from his waist-band. Before he could fire it though, the Indians were crashing into them. A deafening clamour went up from the soldiers. They were standing fully exposed now, waving their guns and some were even running toward the embattled Mormons. They dared not shoot except at lagging Indians.

The melee became general. Lew cocked and fired his gun without consciousness. The acrid smoke stung his eyes. There was an even stronger smell of animal grease and sour sweat. Indians.

He heard someone howling wildly close by and fought with the din in his ears—and never knew it was he, himself, matching the most depraved scream of any savage.

The Mormons broke. The Indians went through their line with momentum and Lew took the advantage the manœuvre gave him. He sunk in his spurs and brandished his pistol and lit out with a thunderous roar, down the line of his men, heading toward the distant hills. The Mormons milled, then broke off and streaked after him. Some were riding horses frantic from pain. Arrow shafts rose and fell, rose and fell, with the undulating stride and the maddened animals found a primitive release from their panic in flight. Men went past Lew unable to stop their horses. He urged them on and rode twisted in his saddle, firing at the Indians.

The pursuit was slow in gathering, but it came. Lew watched as the sweating Indians screamed mightily at one another. He saw the squatty, nearly naked warrior harangue them and point with his bow at the fleeing Mormons, then at the forted-up soldiers. Whatever he said must have sounded logical to his men, because most of them drummed brutally against their lathered horses' ribs and lit out behind him. Lew smiled through the watery feel of his burning eyes. Very deliberately he aimed at the howling warrior in the lead and fired. The Indian ducked as though the ball had gone close enough to his head for him to hear it, but that was all.

The strategy Lew had perfected was sound. The Mormon horses, even those that were wounded, were strong and full of power. They ran belly-down, widening the breach between them and the oncoming savages. Lew swung forward on his horse and peered anxiously into the cylinder of his pistol. One ball left. He looped the reins, filled his mouth with lead balls from his shot pouch, yanked up his powder horn and re-loaded on the run, spitting in balls over powder and working the load-set under the barrel of his pistol until the thing was primed and ready again.

The trees loomed nearer. He worked with sweating hands

145

and kept a sharp lookout on the pursuit. Arrows flew past them, but the danger of being hit wasn't great. Some arrows began to fall short and Lew grinned at that. He looked farther back. The soldiers were small in the distance. The sun glinted off their equipment. He recalled seeing civilians among them. Several men in emigrant dress and two or three others in fringed clothing like Indians wore. Strangely, too, some of the Army's horses were standing up. The motions of the troopers were eloquent in itself although no sound carried from them.

Someone up ahead went down in a wild flurry of hooves. Lew couldn't tell whether the horse or his rider had been hit. He started to rein over when something thick and burly jammed across in front of him, swooping low. He recognised his cousin only by the shock of dark hair and the fleeting glimpse of a face. Then he was lost in the dust, but only long enough for him to emerge on the far side of it with a man dangling by the scruff of his neck from one of Caleb's powerful arms. He spurred up closer. The man was big; too heavy for Cal to lift but not too heavy for him to hold. Lew bent low and used his right hand. Together they got the man up behind Cal on Melissa's powerful chestnut horse.

When Lew stepped heavily in his left stirrup to straighten himself, he saw Danton Mills riding beside him with a wide grin and a purple swelling over one eye. Danton yelled something but Lew couldn't understand it. He smiled broadly, then swung back.

The Indians were, oddly enough, gaining. Apparently they were putting everything left in their mounts into one last race to catch the fleeing Mormons before they got into the protection of the foothills. Lew held his fire but bent lower. The arrows were coming closer. He urged the black horse with knee pressure and stared out through the swirl of men and horses. The trees were getting close. He counted the seconds until he gauged they were all within rifle range, then he straightened up in the saddle, threw back his head and yelled as loudly as he could.

"Scatter, men. Spread out. Give the boys up ahead a chance."

The cry was taken up and repeated. The Mormons shot wild looks over their shoulders, then broke away. They were yelling as they did it. A high, lilting, exultant yell. Lew was watching the Indians. Perhaps the screams of the Mormons unnerved them; possibly some of them had seen movement ahead in the underbrush and from behind the trees; at any rate they yanked back on their single war-bridle reins. It was too late. They were fully exposed and amassed before the lowering forest.

The stunning, ragged fusillade came mushrooming out of the forest's fringe with a shaggy, dirty grey cloud behind it. The smoke seemed to hang. Lew reined his horse up and let him stand. He watched the disintegration of the fighting Indians.

They were caught flat-footed by his strategem. The carnage was awful. Horses and men were in a heap of threshing, gory froth. The howls and cries were soul-wrenching. His cold anger seeped out with the cries of the injured and the sight of the dying. He turned his horse and motioned for the Mormons who had fled with him, to come in closer.

Cal and Danton came with the others. Their faces were grime streaked, flushed and tight looking. The men back in the trees began to yell for their horses. Men rode out of Lew's band to help the horse guards handle the excited animals. The Indians were howling and milling and Lew couldn't find the nearly naked buck among them anywhere. They acted leaderless. He shouted for his men to mount-up. They did. There were stragglers, as always, but he didn't wait for them.

"Once more, boys—hard!"

He had no stomach for it but he led them. They roared

down at the beaten savages in a tattered line with a deafening roar from triumphant throats. The Indians had a moment's glance, then the gunfire made their minds up for them. Abandoning their dead and dying, they turned and fled. It was a shambling flight on stumbling, bloody-eyed horses. Lew swung his horse sideways to halt the flow of his men. He held his arm aloft and yelled at them. They slowed and came to a grinding halt. The silence came down, then. Frightful with the moanings of the dying Indians and the shrill screams, rasping and maddened, from their horses.

Lew swung his horse out around the welter of savages and animals, then reined up and saw Danton wipe his face with a ragged sleeve. "Dan, can you do anything for them?"

Danton regarded the mass of bodies, human and animal. He sucked in a huge breath and nodded his head as he let it out. "I reckon, Lew. Give me some men. I'll try."

"Take what you want."

Faint shouts arose into the spanking afternoon sunlight. Lew swung and looked out over the desert. The soldiers were streaming towards them. The Indians were going southwest at a rambling trot, the best they could get out of horses ridden down to the wind-broke point. And far off, away from all the human activity, the sun was a gigantic ball, blood-red and scouring the desert with its dying brilliance.

Caleb reined up beside him on Melissa's chestnut horse. "Lew, it worked. It worked better'n we could've hoped for."

Lew looked into his cousin's face. There was the same liquid softness to Cal's gaze. The same directness to his glance Aunt Jem had had. He nodded in silence and gathered the black horse's reins in his fist. "I reckon, Cal."

"This is the worst part of it, isn't it?"

Lew nodded, seeing Danton and others of the Mormons tugging dead Indian horses off of dying men; straightening out the limbs of the dead and kneeling over the badly wounded. He heard the shouts of the soldiers getting closer. There was a darkness riding his spirit. He looked over at Caleb. "Well, I've got a little chore to do, Cal, then I'll be back."

He rode away from them, back toward the wagons. Up across the long lilt of the land toward the foothills. The smell of gunpowder was thick in the still atmosphere.

He rode without looking back until he saw a little band of men riding in a Red River cart down from the tight wagon circle, then he swung his reins loose, twisted and watched it move southwest from him. Go down toward the battlefield. It would be a hospital cart. That thought jarred him. She might be in it. Probably was; well, in that case he'd just wait for her to get back. A man didn't have to do any more than wait, really, when things had to be done. Ride and wait. He had learned about patience and waiting years back.

He saw the wagon circle with its bee-hive activity. The faces peering and the dull glint of red sunlight off guns. A slap of woodsmoke went across his face. It was a good smell. A tired man with lead in his heart would always find it so when he rode back. They called to him as he rode up and someone said something about "that arrer." He didn't distinguish—couldn't, exactly—but he heard it said often enough. Old Jakob Mortonson reached with a bony hand and held his horse's cheekpiece. He looked down into the weary old glance and remembered a time when he's seen fire in Jakob's stare. That was a lifetime gone, now. Back in Brazo Valley where the Bullards lay.

"Boy; I'll he'p you with that arrer."

It was becoming something that irked him. "What arrow? What are you talking about?"

Jakob looked at him with a startled, quick. sharp glance, then his grey eyes looked ashamed, a little. " Why, that arrer you got through the calf o' yer leg, Lew. There—that arrer."

There was absolutely no pain. No sensation at all until he was off the saddle and standing on both his legs, and even then he was only subconsciously aware of a hurt in his leg. It was a small thing. The kind of a " kink *" a man gets from being too long in the saddle. What made him look though, was the slipperiness of his foot inside the boot.

" Well—I'll be damned. It *is* an arrow, Jakob."

The old man handed him his long rifle with the same odd look. "Grip 'er tight, boy. As tight as you can. Here; Marsh and Ezra—you too, Cyrus—hold the boy. Hold him tight now."

Then—the pain came—but not until then. The pain like a red-hot prod-pole being run through the muscles of his leg. He could feel the sweat jump out over his body. Could feel its sting in his eyes and taste it salty-bitter in his mouth. And he gripped Jakob's old long rifle hard; so hard his arms shook and his knuckles were white, then grey and bloodless. There was a shaky sigh from the ground. Jakob stood up with his hands bloody, holding a stubby little Comanche war-arrow. He looked into Lew's face, holding the thing in his hands as if he meant to strangle the life out of it.

"Cyrus : you still got a dram o' that bitteroot medicine? Give the boy a swallow."

It wasn't bitteroot medicine at all. It was corn whiskey and it burned like all the fires of hell all the way down, then it kindled its own fury in Lew's entrails somewhere. He gasped and felt the water start into his eyes, but the nausea passed and only the searing anguish in his belly remained. Jakob was holding up the arrow.

" Take it. When I was a boy we used to save 'em. The

ones we lived out. Take it an' go over to the hospital wagon. Missey's over there waiting for the wagon to fetch back the hurt."

He shook off the gnarled fists that would have helped him, but he didn't speak. There was a curling sickness down where the green whiskey lay. He was afraid to agitate it. There was a little anguish in walking, but when he went high on the ball of the wounded foot, the leg only ached a little. Like that he crossed the compound without knowing that he was a centre of hundreds of stares; not caring.

She was standing before a high front wheel with her hands behind her gripping tightly to a rough, scarred old hub, watching him come with the ridiculous and bloody arrow in his fist. Her face was expressionless. The only movement was something dark in the background of her eyes. When he was close she nodded at a cask beside her.

"Sit down there."

He sat, still clutching the arrow. A warmth was spreading out in him. She knelt and pushed up his trouser leg. "Hold it," she said colourlessly; he did. She looked at the purpling, swelling holes and pursed her mouth. He watched her face instead of looking at his wound. "You'll have to wear a poultice, Lew."

Then he spoke. "All right, ma'm. You fix it an' I'll wear it."

She gazed up at him, saw the ruddy flush in his face and the warm sparkle in his eyes. Saw a boldness there she had never seen before, and raised herself up slowly, bent low before his face and wrinkled her nose, then straightened all the way up with a funny little frown. "What did you drink—over there?"

"Why, your paw said it was bitteroot medicine, Melissa. You know I'd not question a man like your paw."

The little frown faded and a strange, guilty shaft of

humour showed. "You haven't eaten anything all day, have you?"

"Why—no, ma'm. Now that I think on it, I don't reckon I have."

She fought against the smile and succeeded, but there was a little pause while she did it. "Lew—the next time one of those old men gives you bitteroot medicine—just take a small swallow of it. Don't gulp it down."

"Yes'm. Just a little swig." His eyes never blinked. The warmth in them was soft and liquid-looking. The dryness, the hard tension, was gone altogether. She returned his steady look with one just as steady.

"Lew, how many were hurt out there?"

"I don't rightly know, Missy. I—well—I just didn't stay to see. There's a wagon gone out. They'll fetch them all back."

"Was it bad?"

"Pretty bad, ma'm. Pretty bad."

"We could see what our men did. Whose idea was that —splitting up the Saints and leading the heathen back to them?"

"Why—it was my idea, ma'm."

"You did it again, didn't you?"

His face was slack, almost dumb-looking. "I reckon I must've, if you say so." Then he scowled a little. A slight darkening came into his glance. Something stirred in his soul; a thickening of spirit. "Did what, ma'm?"

"Saved the Mormons—saved the soldiers. Saved lives, I mean. Proved there's a blessing in you, not a curse."

The confusion in him swelled. It was a baffling, tearing feeling. Almost a crumbling feeling. Surely it was a weakened sensation. He dropped his gaze for a moment to the wounded leg, thought vaguely that the loss of blood made him feel that way, then lifted up his eyes to her face again and licked his lips, but said nothing. The warmth

152

flowed steadily, evenly, in his blood. His deep, remembering blood . . .

Melissa bent slowly, as though compelled to it. She took his dirty face in both of her hands and tilted it back. He made no resistance. She kissed him. Squarely on the mouth. Right flush on the mouth.

He was dumbfounded, petrified with astonishment. Then the bitteroot medicine of Jakob Mortonson came to his aid. He kissed her right back.

She laughed. The sound went rippling over the drab bivouac with its minor bedlam. Its barking of dogs and stamping of hooves and drone of people talking. It lifted over and above the grim sounds of an embattled people triumphant and shuffling their feet, waiting—waiting— waiting to count their cost. A soft, rich sound carried away.

"Lew, you're drunk. Do you know that? You're drunk."

"Why," he said sonorously, "I reckon not, ma'm." Then the realisation of the truth was borne in upon him with a sense of horror. He looked at her and clenched his fists— one with an arrow in it; a bloody arrow from a Comanche war-bow—and he very firmly stood up. Then—the pain came. Real livid, breathtaking pain. He bore down against it with his teeth, but a tiny groan worked its way through.

"Lew! Sit down!"

He sat for the second time and she hurried toward the hospital wagon without looking at him again. He held the leg out in front of him and waited. When she came back she had rags and a wooden bowl and a wisp of taffy hair hanging over her forehead that she jutted her lower lip and blew at. She went to work with the poultice. He watched her, unaware of the noise the people were making until the ground thudded near him; then he looked up. Elder Mortonson was standing there. His fixed, stern glance was on Melissa more than Lew. She worked on oblivious. Lew studied the strong jaw and the great shock of grey-streaked hair.

"Elder—something I sent Cal to find out and never got a chance to ask him about afterwards. Just how far are we from Zion?"

Mortonson's eyes moved away from Melissa's head slowly. There was disapproval in them that held even when he looked at Lew. "Zion? We've this desert to cross. That's all, Lewis. Just this desert. We're almost there. Three to five days, then Zion."

Lew dropped his glance. He saw the hospital wagon coming and the dying sunlight flaming red along its sides. "How many hurt—how many dead?"

"We have none dead, Lewis. Seven hurt. Two badly. Eight hurt counting you. That was good fighting. There's an Army officer over at the drinking cask. He said you saved every one of them and our men, too, by working it that way."

Lew looked across the compound. There was a straggle of filthy soldiers trailing in the wake of the mounted men. All of them coming now, behind the wagonload of injured. "A soldier? Well—I expect I'll go see him."

Melissa looked up with her fierce glance. "You'll stay right here." She shot her uncle a long look with defiance in it. "Bring him over here."

" Melissa—" the deep-booming voice rolled out like a clap of thunder. " Your father told me what he saw you do to Lewis, here. Have you no shame, girl? Here—like this? Everyone will know by morning, girl."

Lew's anger came with its swift-running fierceness. " Elder—I did that. If you want to lay blame, then lay it here."

Mortonson's glance swung solidly to Lew's face. Their eyes locked. Melissa got up swiftly, there was a soaring, deep-mantling russet under her skin. " Uncle, leave him be. If that's the best the people of this train can offer him for all he's done—God knows it's a poor reward!"

Mortonson's mouth drew inward. The sternness lay thick and solid in his glance, but he said nothing. He never got the chance, for the clanking of great, curved sabres, a totally unfamiliar sound to all of them, interrupted. Lew looked at the officer. He was a wan looking man, lean to the point of emaciation with hot, dark eyes veiled in bone-weariness and a touch of grey at the temples. But he had a good smile and he used it now.

"You're the leader, aren't you? I recognise you by your clothing."

"No," Lew said softly, curtly, rolling his head sideways to indicate Elder Mortonson. "This is our leader. Elder Mortonson."

The smile stayed. There was an intentness to the soldier's dark glance. "No, I know Elder Mortonson. We met out there. No, I mean the leader of those Mormons who came out and worked that ambushing trick on those Comanches."

Lew didn't know what to say so he remained silent. Melissa spoke quickly. "Yes; he was the one. He planned it. That isn't all he's done, either."

"Melissa!"

She looked at him and lowered her head a little, regarded the poultice dressing, bent low and went to work on it again, but her hands shook. The officer clasped his hands behind his back and rocked back a little. His dark eyes never left Lew's face. There was a glow of admiration in them.

"You should have made the Army your calling, mister."

Lew's smile was crooked. "Never had a chance to," he said. The inner warmth was fading now and the wound burned with an unholy painfulness. "How come you soldiers to be way out here, like that?"

"Well, I'm from Fort Defiance down in the Arizona

Territory. We came up here because we got orders to bring back a renegade Mormon named Landsborough. Fact is, there's a sheriff Mueller from St. Joseph, over on the Missouri river, who's along because he's the only man in the country who can recognise this outlaw."

"You came a long way," Lew said softly. "That's a funny thing about the law. I told my cousin that one time. It'll never let an outlaw rest; never."

"There has to be law," the officer said. He smiled then and wagged his head a little. "Out here the distances make it hard to keep—but we're trying. The men with me—they all wanted me to thank you very sincerely for them. We heard down at Escalon Outpost there were Comanche raiding parties in the Utah country this spring. Never thought they'd be that strong, though."

Lew felt the tightness of the bandage. He looked down and was caught in Melissa's pleading glance. He understood only part of what she was trying to say with her eyes, but it was enough. He looked away again—and froze.

There were three civilians of the Army's party threading their way through the arising cooking fires. The one in the middle, the one with the red, stiff rag around his upper arm and the sleeve cut away from his flesh, was Sheriff Mueller. He remembered him well. The wispy hair, the dour, glum look, the grey complexion and still eyes.

"Here comes part of your outfit," Lew said softly.

The officer turned and watched the men come closer. Melissa stood up with her fingers interlaced, her face white and the troubled depths of her eyes a deep, almost violet colour.

"Yes. The one in the middle with the bandaged arm, that's Sheriff Mueller of St. Joseph. The man they sent to help us. The only one in the country who'd recognise this outlaw, Landsborough."

"Yeah," Lew said dryly, watching the men come up.

Elder Mortonson cleared his throat. Lew glanced at him, followed the hard glint of his rugged profile and saw the way some Mormon men were coming stealthily through the swift-gathering gloom, blocking off the firelight with their numbers. It made his heart miss a beat. He could identity several figures among the nearing silhouettes. Danton Mills; Cal, Charley Crawford; farther back—old Jakob clutching the long old rifle. Lew straightened up on the keg he was sitting on. His breath went out of him in tight little gasps. The voice of the officer interrupted the thickening silence like a jarring tremor.

" Sheriff, this is the man who led them. There—the one on the cask."

Lew was waiting. Mueller's eyes went to his face. Lew waited. There was just the barest flicker, once, fleetingly, then the lids drooped to their habitual squint and the grey eyes held a touch of sardonic irony in them. Mueller spoke and the words came slowly, very distinctly.

" We're beholden to you, Mister." Lew was held still by the blankness, the dimly seen ironic wisp of secretive amusement in the grey glance that never wavered, never blinked. Mueller paused. " Seems like you Mormons are pretty handy at savin' lives. One of you pulled me out of the Missouri river year or such a matter back." Mueller relaxed and shuffled his feet but his glance was like lead; heavy and unmoving and inwardly thoughtful.

" Had a feller with me then. Feller named Gerrit. He got killed in a gunfight when we crossed back over the river. Too bad about him dyin' like that—he deserved better."

Lew was as rigid as the rest of them. Mueller appeared in no hurry. The army officer was glancing around at the men who were standing behind them all; the wall of hard faces with unmoving eyes. " Mueller," he said, " did you walk among them like you said you were going to?"

" Yep, Captain, sure did."

157

"Did you see him? Is this the band he was with?"

Mueller's steady glance never moved, but his head did, back and forth a little. " No; that renegade Landsborough isn't in this camp, Captain." He paused, looking straight at Lew. " I've never seen any of these people before in my life. This man here, too; he's a perfect stranger to me."

Lew let the air out faster. He wasn't conscious of the grip he had on the rim of the little keg until someone coughed, cleared his throat, spat, then spoke out of the lowering darkness behind them all. It was Jakob; Lew knew the voice.

"If you fellers're ready, I expect you can eat now."

The tension was broken. The officer's smile came up again. " Here come the litters, Miss—I reckon you'll be busy. I've got some aidmen; I'll send them over to you."

Lew got up. The pain was there, sharper, perhaps, more fiery and throbbing. He took a step that cost him a lot, but he took it anyway, and held out his hand, low. " Glad to meet you, sheriff," he said.

Mueller looked down at the hand, then very slowly took it in his own fist and pumped it gently once. His sardonic gaze was easy and steely looking. He dropped Lew's fingers and waited until the sounds of men walking away were dim and soft, then he spoke again. " Too bad about Gerrit, isn't it?"

" I reckon," Lew said softly. " A man learns, though."

" You wouldn't have gone back for him anyway, would you?"

" No, I wouldn't have."

" All right. You saved my hide twice, Landsborough. I owed you this—especially now—this close to Zion." He hooked his thumbs in his shell-belt. The sardonic look remained. " Don't ever come back."

" I never will. That's all past, sheriff."

" I thought so, that's why I didn't recognise you. No one's perfect—damned few are brave. You've got a new

158

start; I'm hoping for you. And, by the way, save me embarrassment and change your name, will you?"

"Sure. And—well, just thanks, I reckon."

Mueller shook his head. "No thanks. I just plain didn't recognise you is all. No thanks for a bad memory."

Mueller turned stiffly, wearily, and walked away. Lew stood with the throbbing agony shooting up from his leg and wasn't conscious of anything until a small hand plucked at his arm.

"Lew?"

He looked down into her face. It was highlighted by the little fires low on the ground. "Yes'm?"

"I can't spare but a minute. They've brought in the wounded. Lew; do you believe what we've all been trying to tell you for so long—now?"

He nodded at her soberly. "I reckon I do, Melissa. There isn't any curse any more, is there?"

"No. There's a new world and a new life for you, though."

"I can't hardly believe it, Melissa." He looked over the busy camp and the night-hush beyond, then turned fully towards her. "Melissa?"

"Yes?"

"I—well—I don't want to start out alone; a man gets awfully lonely sometimes; especially one that's been alone so much." He reached for her, found her arms and she didn't move away from him. Then a fear came into him that was something new. A fear of saying the wrong thing —of doing something he shouldn't. He let his hands drop away. "I—well; I'm new at this. Will you sort of let me figure out the right words? The right way of doing this—this proposing business, Melissa?"

"Yes; I'll wait, Lew. I'm good at waiting." Then she moved a little closer and stood on her tiptoes. "This is good-night; I'm going to be terribly busy until tomorrow." She kissed him again.

Lauran Paine who, under his own name and various pseudonyms has written over 900 books, was born in Duluth, Minnesota, a descendant of the Revolutionary War patriot and author, Thomas Paine. His family moved to California when he was at an early age and his apprenticeship as a Western writer came about through the years he spent in the livestock trade, rodeos, and even motion pictures where he served as an extra because of his expert horsemanship in several films starring movie cowboy Johnny Mack Brown. In the late 1930s, Paine trapped wild horses in Northern Arizona and even, for a time, worked as a professional farrier. Paine came to know the Old West through the eyes of many who had been born in the previous century and he learned that Western life had been very different from the way it was portrayed on the screen. "I knew men who had killed other men," he later recalled. "But they were the exceptions. Prior to and during the Depression, people were just too busy eking out an existence to indulge in Saturday-night brawls." He served in the U.S. Navy in the Second World War and began writing for Western pulp magazines following his discharge. It is interesting to note that all of his earliest novels (written under his own name and the pseudonym Mark Carrel) were published in the British market and he soon had as strong a following in that country as in the United States. Paine's Western fiction is characterized by strong plots, authenticity, an apparently effortless ability to construct situation and character, and a preference for building his stories upon a solid foundation of historical fact. *Abode Empire* (1956), one of his best novels, is a fictionalized account of the last twenty years in the life of trader William Bent and, in an off-trail way, has a melancholy, bittersweet texture that is not easily forgotten. *Moon Prairie* (1950), first published in the United States in 1994, is a memorable story set during the mountain man period of the frontier. In later novels such as *The Homesteaders* (1986) or *The Open Range Men* (1990), he showed that the special magic and power of his stories and characters had only matured along with his basic themes of changing times, changing attitudes, learning from experience, respecting nature, and the yearning for a simpler, more moderate way of life. His most recent Western novels have been published as Five Star Westerns and include *Tears of the Heart*, *Lockwood* and *The White Bird*.